All about the author...
Caitlin Crews

CAITLIN CREWS discovered her ~~first~~ ... ~~twe~~lve. It involved swashbuckling pirates, grand ad~~ventures~~ ... ~~ski~~rts and a mind of her own, and a seriously mouth~~y~~ ... ~~her~~o. The book (the title of which remains lost in the mists of ~~the~~ *at the age of* ~~furi~~ous impression. Caitlin was immediately smitten with roman~~ces~~ and romance heroes, to the detriment of her middle school social life. And so began her lifelong love affair with romance novels, many of which she insists on keeping near her at all times.

Caitlin has made her home in places as far-flung as York, England, and Atlanta, Georgia. She was raised near New York City, and fell in love with London on her first visit when she was a teenager. She has backpacked in Zimbabwe, been on safari in Botswana and visited tiny villages in Namibia. She has, while visiting the place in question, declared her intention to live in Prague, Dublin, Paris, Athens, Nice, the Greek Islands, Rome, Venice and/or any of the Hawaiian islands. Writing about exotic places seems like the next best thing to moving there.

She currently lives in California with her animator/comic book artist husband and their menagerie of ridiculous animals.

* * *

"Crews' pulse-pounding, sensual feast of a page-turner keeps the heat turned up in this unforgettable, love-em, hate-em romance. She showcases luxurious settings, while her awe-inspiring couple entertains with their sexual banter and some of the most jaw-dropping lovemaking ever written."
—*RT Book Reviews* on *A Scandal in the Headlines*

"Crews' tale is intensely dramatic, set in a quaint fictional European principality. The royal repartee is all-consuming, their lovemaking is sensual and volatile and their romance is a nightmare turned fairy tale."
—*RT Book Reviews* on *A Royal Without Rules*

"Crews' magnificently intense and passion-filled romance is so volatile you'll feel the heat radiating from her couple, who trade barbs and ignite sparks right into the bedroom."
—*RT Book Reviews* on *No More Sweet Surrender*

"Crews' scorching love scenes and cryptic hints will keep readers rapt as she pieces her puzzle together, with a couple who truly deserves happiness."
—*RT Book Reviews* on *Heiress Behind the Headlines*

"Crews' modern-day *Beauty and the Beast* story comes alive with a hero and heroine who are both so much more than they seem."
—*RT Book Reviews* on *The Man Behind the Scars*

CAITLIN CREWS

scandalize me

H **HARLEQUIN** PRESENTS®

Recycling programs
for this product may
not exist in your area.

ISBN-13: 978-0-373-43038-3

SCANDALIZE ME

Copyright © 2014 by Harlequin Books S.A.

Special thanks and acknowledgment are given to Caitlin Crews for her contribution
to the *Fifth Avenue* trilogy.

This edition published by arrangement with Harlequin Books S.A.

For questions and comments about the quality of this book, please contact us
at CustomerService@Harlequin.com.

Printed in U.S.A.

scandalize me

Chapter One

Zoe Brook strode into the exclusive strip club, hidden away beneath a discreet sign on a side street in an otherwise upscale Manhattan neighborhood, like an avenging angel on the warpath at last.

It had taken almost seven years, but her revenge was within grasp.

At last.

She paid no attention to the dull-eyed bouncers who waved her through the doorway, much less the plastic smile of the hostess as she swept past the welcome desk. There were very few clients at this hour of the morning—10:17, last she'd checked—and that made it easy to find who she was looking for in the dimly lit, too-loud space, dotted here and there with the requisite poles and a handful of sleepy-looking dancers eking out halfhearted performances in the dark red gloom.

Not that her quarry was making any attempt to hide.

Hunter Talbot Grant III, one-time golden boy, dumb jock extraordinaire and current professional fuckup, sprawled on a plush booth in the corner of the otherwise sparsely populated club, neck deep in mostly naked women. Zoe's lips thinned as she took in the scene, which was as distasteful as she'd expected. The women giggled on each side of him, they shimmied in front of him, they writhed for his pleasure as if his table was its own stage and Zoe, dressed in her usual sleek sort of sheath dress and a tailored coat against the winter chill, was wearing more clothing than all of them put together.

"Good morning, Mr. Grant," she said crisply, eying the man himself in all his sordid glory. "You seem to have forgotten our nine-thirty meeting today."

It wasn't exactly a *surprise* that someone who currently ranked as the Most Hated Celebrity in America was a pig. In fact, Zoe was counting on it. Hunter Grant was the disgraced sports figure du jour, wealthy beyond measure and disreputable by choice, and strip clubs such as this one were his natural habitat. *Pig* was redundant.

"And you seem to be wearing entirely too many clothes."

His voice was a rough growl, deeply male and shot through with raw, velvet arrogance, which went with his very big, undeniably impressive body sprawled there in the booth, dripping with strippers. But he met her gaze as if they were alone and he was entirely sober, and there was suddenly a certain hum in the air, a kind of electric charge, that made her skin feel much too tight.

She ignored the odd sensation, keeping her gaze on him as if the shock of his intense physicality didn't seem to suck the air from all around him like a vacuum. Or as if she simply didn't notice it, because she shouldn't. Because she *couldn't.*

"It's a terrible habit of mine." She let her brows rise in challenge, because he was a man who'd played games for a living, and men like that lived for challenges of all kinds. They couldn't help it. And that meant she could use it against him. "I can't seem to break it."

"I recommend quitting cold turkey," he said with a dark gleam in his famously sky blue eyes, about which whole songs by pop princesses had been written over the years.

Zoe had dutifully downloaded every one of them over the past few weeks as part of her exhaustive research into the life and times and various offensive behaviors of Hunter Grant, the worst-behaved NFL quarterback in recent history. She needed to know every single thing about him if she was going to use him like her own, personal weapon.

And she was. He just didn't know it yet.

"And what have you quit that makes you an expert on the subject?" she asked now. "Besides football, I mean."

"I didn't quit football. I was fired. With extreme prejudice. You can read about it in all the tabloids."

"I'm thinking, then, that maybe you're not the best person in the world to talk to about quitting things."

Hunter's mouth curved. "I don't give a shit what you quit or don't quit, honey. But I'd like you a whole lot better if you were naked."

It was a pity he was even more attractive in person, Zoe

thought then. It was that careless dark blond hair that never seemed to be fully tamed no matter how short he cut it. That gorgeous face of his, with eyes that should have been pretty and high cheekbones that should have been fey, but somehow worked with that pugnacious jaw of his to make him decidedly, almost alarmingly masculine, despite the offensive things he said.

Zoe knew every inch of his famous face, that well-documented smirk, and most of that much-photographed body of his, that today—or last night, more likely—he'd shoved into faded jeans and a tight gray Henley that hugged his rangy male form. He would have been a tabloid favorite anyway because of his wealthy family background, his all-American good looks and his penchant for vapid yet beautiful starlets—but it was his half brat, half thug behavior on the football field that had kept him plastered across every glossy magazine in existence for the rocky decade that had made up his football career.

He's nothing but a frat boy, she thought, smiling at him as if she liked him. Pretty as a picture with malice and entitlement beneath, like all the rest of his kind. She knew. She'd been there a decade ago when he'd proved exactly what kind of man he was. She didn't expect him to remember that, but then, she didn't want him to remember her.

Not yet.

Not until he did what she needed him to do and helped her take down Jason Treffen.

"Looked your fill?"

His voice wasn't friendly or polite, and he didn't flash that absurdly charming smile she'd seen him wield throughout the series of insincere mea culpas he'd issued after each of his many scandals as a football star. He only watched her, in a curiously intent way that made her feel as if she ought to hold her breath.

"I'm not admiring you," Zoe said coolly, and she wasn't. Of course she wasn't.

"Don't you think you should?" His voice was as lazy as ever but still, she heard the challenge in it. The thrown gauntlet—because, as expected, he couldn't resist. "I'm usually the object of intense and potentially life-altering admiration. It's but one of my many burdens to bear."

She was surprised that some part of her wanted to laugh at the way he said that, with that sardonic lash that suggested he was far more self-aware than she'd imagined. But she didn't know what to do with that, so instead of exploring it, she got down to business. She dug into her bag, opened her wallet and handed her credit card to the nearest dancer, not looking away from Hunter until the other woman took it from her fingers.

"Take this. Take them. And don't let anyone come back over here unless I say it's okay," she ordered her.

She stared at the dancer until the woman did as she was told with only a quick glance at Hunter, herding the pack of strippers out of Hunter's booth with a single jerk of her head.

"It's like you're my fairy godmother," he said when they were left alone, a hint of a drawl in his voice, reminding her he'd spent the past decade in Texas. If possible, he seemed even lazier than before now that there was only him in the booth. And, somehow, bigger. "But I'm all grown up now. I can pay for my own strippers."

Zoe settled herself on the seat next to him so she could turn toward him, the better to quietly block him in where he sat. The gleam in his gaze told her he knew exactly what she was doing. That he let her do it. She ignored the gleam.

"Congratulations, Mr. Grant," she said crisply. "This is your lucky day."

"It felt a lot luckier five minutes ago, *before* you scared off all the half-naked women."

"I set up an appointment through your manager, but it appears you prefer to operate through more casual channels these days."

"If that's a convoluted way of saying I told Harvey to go fuck himself, you are correct."

Zoe smiled. Harvey Speer was a frothing bulldog of a sports agent, well-known for creating insurmountable barriers between his clients and the world, so she'd hardly weep salty tears if he wasn't involved in Hunter's life any longer. It made what she wanted to do with him that much easier.

"I'm Zoe Brook," she told him now. "You really should know that already. I'm the best PR agent in New York City, if not the whole world, and I'm going to rehabilitate your image—which I think we can both agree is more than a little tarnished."

He eyed her for a long moment, and she was sure she saw

something hollow move through his gaze, stark and almost painful, completely at odds with the shallow, degenerate man she knew he'd been all his life. But then his mouth kicked up in one corner, his eyes shone blue and clear, and she was certain she'd imagined it.

"I'll pass," he said. She had the strangest notion that he was dangerous, suddenly, which was absurd, but he never moved that unnervingly direct gaze from hers. "Send some of those strippers back over here on your way out, won't you?"

She let her smile go sharp. "You misunderstand me. I'm not asking you if you'd like me to do it. I'm telling you that I will."

"Is this a fan thing?" he asked, his voice still mild but his gaze intent. "Some stalker fantasy? Knock yourself out. Rehab away. But please don't expect me to have anything to do with it. I like my notoriety just fine the way it is."

Zoe laughed. "Oh, I'm not a fan."

"It's okay to admit it. I have a lot of fans, even now. Some of them like to make up complicated little stories to get close to me, and I don't really mind. I don't care who you are. But then again, I don't much care who *I* am, either."

"Let's be honest, shall we, Mr. Grant?"

"By all means. All this flattery is making me dizzy. Of course, I'm drunk."

Except she didn't think he was. His gaze was too sharp, there were no bottles on the table, and she was sitting so close to him that if there'd been any alcohol on his breath, she'd have been able to smell it. Why would he want her to think he was drunk if he wasn't? She shook that off, then leaned in, her smile hard.

"You have the kind of throwing arm that makes strong, silent men weep tears of joy, yet you've treated it shabbily and without the slightest respect throughout your career," she said coolly. "Your bad behavior is legendary and you quite possibly lost your team the Super Bowl this year. On top of that, you were—literally, it's rumored—born with a silver spoon stuck in your patrician mouth as the heir to the great Grant fortune, meaning no one is ever likely to sympathize with you. About anything."

"The rumors are wrong." His smile was bland. "Unless you mean the sort of silver spoon more commonly used to snort large quantities of cocaine. Those we pass down during our strange puberty rituals, one stuffy WASP to the next. The first exchange took place on the *Mayflower,* I think. It's a genetic imperative at this point."

Zoe was surprised that she wanted to smile at that bit of nonsense. Possibly even laugh. But surely that was weakness, and she didn't allow any of that. Not any longer. Certainly not with someone like him, who wasn't high on cocaine any more than he was drunk, but apparently wanted to be thought both.

But she wasn't here to understand him, only to use him.

"You could have sailed straight into some investment bank after Harvard and played with all of your Monopoly money for the rest of your life like your father and grandfather before you, but you opted for professional football instead, to the enduring dismay of your snooty, upper-crust relatives. Everyone expected you'd be crushed as a rookie, but instead, you dominated. You should be one of the great success stories of the age, an athlete with an Ivy League—trained mind. A role model for our time." She eyed him, not making the slightest effort to hide her disdain. "A hero among men."

"Sadly," Hunter said, and though his smile never wavered, she was sure that she saw something dark move over his face again before he hid it, "I'm only me. Though my wasted potential haunts me, I promise."

That wasn't darkness, Zoe told herself firmly. That was emptiness. He was nothing but a pretty shell wrapped tight around nothing at all. Which was precisely why she'd chosen him to push the repulsive Jason Treffen where she wanted him, at last. She'd spent a few hellish years under Jason's control, and she remembered three men in particular from that long-ago December night that had convinced her she had to save herself or die. Jason's own son, Austin, now a lawyer like his evil father. Alex Diaz, now an investigative reporter. And Hunter, the rich and pretty football player, clearly not the brains of the trio. She'd decided that now she was finally ready to do what needed to be done, Hunter would be the easiest to manipulate. Obviously.

"I doubt that very much," she said now, her voice light, though her stare was anything but, and she was surprised he returned it so steadily. That he didn't so much as flinch.

"You're more likely than not a complete and utter blank, straight through to your benighted soul. One shade up from sociopathic, if I had to guess. The good news is this makes you a perfect candidate for a high-profile corporate position, which I'm assuming has to be your next move. Or let me rephrase that. It should be, and I can help you achieve that."

"I'll hand it to you..." She thought that smile of his sharpened, that there was more of that temper there, just behind the blue of his eyes as he leaned in closer as if he was sharing his secrets. "This is certainly a unique approach."

It was the age-old carrot-and-stick routine, in fact, and he shouldn't seem so aware of it yet simultaneously unruffled by it. Zoe forged on.

"It's the transition from football-field temper tantrum to corporate dominance that needs to be refined," she continued, still sounding so airy and easy, despite the fact this wasn't going quite how she'd imagined it would. "What you need to learn is how to hide your true face better."

"I don't hide my true face at all," he said, and there was something quietly devastating in the way he said it. It struck Zoe like a blow, low and hard, and she didn't know why. "What would be the point? Everyone's already seen it."

Zoe crossed her legs, settling back against her seat as if she, too, was completely relaxed, here in this tawdry place, in the company of a man who should have disgusted her— who *had* disgusted her, and thoroughly, before she'd started talking to him. She ignored that odd pang inside her at the dark look on his face, the leftover echo of that strange blow.

"I find it's better to beware rich and powerful men who are also renowned for their good looks, because they tend to believe their own bullshit and usually don't even know they're lying. And they're always lying, *especially* when they claim to be telling the truth."

He held one hand to his chest, covering the place his heart should have been, had he possessed one. She was skeptical. His mouth curled in one corner, mocking them both. "It's like you know me."

He shifted in his seat then, and she imagined for a moment he was uncomfortable, though there was nothing on his face to suggest it. Just that fierce maleness that was uniquely his, and an odd intensity she couldn't quite place. A strange kind of quiver hummed in her, low and deep, like the echo of a far-off earthquake, stirring up uneasy memories of her dusty, sun-drunk California childhood.

"You're staring at me," he pointed out. "Are you sure you're not a fan? I ask because generally, that's exactly what fans do."

Zoe smiled, and she could feel the sharp edge of it, like the knife it was. She could only hope he did, too.

"I'm calculating the extent of your dissipation," she told him. "There are only so many miracles I can be expected to perform, you understand. Some prospective clients require a few weeks or months in what we euphemistically call *a health spa* before we can even begin to have a sensible conversation about overhauling a tarnished public persona. And yours..." She let the blade of her smile cut deep, then waved a hand between them to indicate their surroundings. "Well. You're rather more rusted through than most, aren't you?"

"I like to think there's no actual structural damage."

His mouth crooked again, though his gaze stayed level on hers, and she knew better, somehow, than to believe him.

"I imagine that depends on what the structure was originally. Or what it was meant to be before all the years of dissolution and decay."

There was the flicker of something unsettling in his too-blue gaze, still oddly intent on hers.

"And here I thought you were the best PR person money could buy," he said softly. "According to your own sales pitch not five minutes ago. Capable of turning any rusted thing into a gleaming, squeaky-clean pillar of the community if you choose."

There was no false modesty in her when she answered simply, "I am."

"That's hard to believe, if this is how you talk to your potential clients. All of whom can't possibly be as laid-back and jovial as me."

"You haven't yet agreed to be my client, Mr. Grant." She let him see the steel behind her smile, her gaze. "But I should warn you that I'm not talking about miracles, here. No one's going to confuse you with the Dalai Lama no matter how brilliant a campaign we run. I'm a PR specialist, not the patron saint of lost causes."

"That would be Saint Jude."

"I'm sorry?"

"Saint Jude. Martyred with an ax a very long time ago, which had to have hurt, or it isn't really martyrdom, is it? And since then, the patron saint of lost causes."

"I wouldn't have pegged you as the religious sort. More the blasphemous, deliberately profane sort, if your personal history and laundry list of paternity suits is any kind of guide."

"Dismissed paternity suits," he corrected her, a faintly chiding note in his voice. "And the fact I know the names of a few saints doesn't make me a believer."

Something hollow moved over his face then, but when Zoe blinked, it was gone, and he looked the way she assumed he always did. Vaguely challenging. Mocking. Arrogant and lazy, as if she'd only imagined he could be anything else, though she hadn't the slightest idea why she seemed to want to do that.

"Doesn't it?" she asked, but she was losing her grip on this conversation the more he watched her, as if she was edible and he was suddenly famished.

"It only makes me widely read." He shrugged. "The more sacred cows you're aware of, I find, the more fun it is to tip them over. One after the next."

"And by 'widely read,' I assume you mean, what? *Playboy* magazine? I hate to break this to you, but I don't think anyone's likely to believe you're in it for the articles."

"I'm more of a doer than a reader, I'll admit." His expression shifted into dark amusement. "Want a demonstration?"

There was a crackle of something then, a kind of sharp, hot pang of awareness, and Zoe reminded herself that she wasn't here to banter with this man. She had a very specific agenda. A plan, and he was nothing more than the perfect tool to execute it. There was no room for anything else. It didn't matter that he was significantly more clever and far less drunk than she'd anticipated.

And besides, she knew exactly what he was. She knew what he'd done. Why was that so difficult to keep in mind now that she was this close to him?

"Do you imagine that I'll be so easily seduced?" she asked, trying to keep her voice more arch than accusatory. "Is that how it normally works for you? You roll out a halfhearted sexual innuendo and they fling themselves at your feet?"

"I hadn't imagined anything of the kind," he said, and he was laughing at her, if only with those unnervingly clear eyes. "But I am now."

"You're not my type," she said, sharp and smooth. "I prefer brains over brawn, for a start."

"I beg your pardon." But he wasn't even remotely offended, she saw. If anything, he looked genuinely amused. It made his gorgeous face lighten, made those eyes of his very nearly shine. "I went to Harvard."

"As did almost every single relative and ancestor you have, stretching back to the Massachusetts Bay Colony in the 1600s." She kept her voice dry. "It's somewhat less impressive to be a legacy times twenty. It would only be note-worthy if you *didn't* go to Harvard."

"I didn't merely get into Harvard," he pointed out, that gleam in his gaze never fading. If anything, it intensified, as if he really was imagining her at his feet, spread out before him like—she stopped herself right there. "I also graduated. That's harder, even for someone with so much Crimson in his bloodstream." He grinned. "Brains *and* brawn."

Zoe shrugged. "I also don't like sports. Especially football. Pointless and brutal little war games dressed up in silly costumes and pretending to be important." She smiled. Sweetly. "No offense, of course. Just my opinion."

"I pride myself on never taking offense at the unsolicited opinions of strangers," Hunter said.

He shifted in his seat again, moving his strong legs beneath the table, making Zoe aware of how close they were sitting. How intimate it really was to be practically cuddled up in a private booth with this man. This terrible man. It took everything she had not to jerk back to a safe distance—but then, this was the game. This was what she had to do to win it. And she *would* win it.

"I was fired from the war games," he confided after a moment. "If that helps."

"And I don't really like WASP-y Sons of the Revolution, either," she said almost sadly. "With blood so blue it practically weeps, who still think the world is their own, personal fiefdom. It's a strange character flaw of mine, I'm sure."

That made him grin. "Given the research you've clearly

done, you must know that I'm the black sheep of my WASP-y, Sons and Daughters of the Revolution family. They sigh heavily whenever they see me, which isn't very often. I'm terribly scandalous."

"Or maybe it's just you, Mr. Grant. I can't say I particularly like *you*."

"And yet here you are," Hunter said, something about that tone making it clear she'd be a fool to underestimate him, though he still grinned with every appearance of pretty-boy ease. "Giving me your sales pitch in a strip club at ten-thirty on a Tuesday morning. Do you know who does things like that, Ms. Brook?" There was something about her name in his mouth, that famously dissipated mouth, that worked inside her, making her feel looser than she should, as if he could melt all the ice and iron within her that easily. She told herself she was horrified at the thought. "Fans and stalkers."

"I promise you, I'm neither."

"Then why on earth would you take on the Herculean task of attempting to restore my good name?" He laughed. "It can't be done."

"I have my reasons. All you have to do is benefit from them."

"Let me guess. The goodness of your heart?"

"I don't have a heart, Mr. Grant. I have a plan. You figure prominently in it, that's all."

That intensity that spiked the air around him tightened then, like an implacable fist. And then he smiled, sending a shot of something silken and ominous down the length of her spine. It occurred to her that she didn't understand this man at all. That her research hadn't prepared her for this, whatever this was. For *him*.

"I'm sorry to disappoint you," he said in a velvet whisper, the way another man might talk of sex and desire, and it shivered inside Zoe like a touch, "but I'm committed to my downward spiral, and that leaves no room for anything else. Certainly not a mysterious woman and her 'plan.'"

He rose to his feet then, in a kind of powerfully sinuous way that reminded her that he'd made his living for most of his life with that steel-hewn body of his. She didn't know why that made her throat go dry, but it did. It bordered on painful.

What was happening to her?

"Feel free to stay and enjoy the show," he said, smirking down at her. "The dancers here are very talented. Don't forget to tip."

Then he started to move past her, headed for the door, dismissing her that easily.

"Wait."

Zoe rose and reached out for him as she spoke, but he saw her and shifted, throwing out one of his remarkable hands— widely held to be miracles in their own right, or so she'd read—to clasp hers in midair. As if they'd choreographed it.

And sensation poured into her, a white, wild heat, turning her to stone where she stood. Turning her body against her. She felt that simple touch like a hammer. It coursed through her, and before she could think better of it, before she could *think,* she jerked her startled gaze from their hands to his face—

And everything sizzled. Bright. Hot. Painful.

Impossible.

Hunter's gaze narrowed. Turned dark.

Hungry.

It took every single bit of hard-won pride and determination Zoe had not to rip her hand out from his much bigger one, to reclaim it, to shut off this insane *thing* that lit her up in the worst possible places, from the hollow of her belly to the secret places below. Behind her knees. The curve of her neck. The suddenly taut and aching crests of her breasts, thankfully hidden behind the thick wool of her dress.

But she didn't kid herself. He knew.

And she hated that she could react like this to a man like him. That her body didn't seem to care what she knew about him. That she'd learned nothing from all these long, hard years. That she simply burned.

"I prefer not to be manhandled, thank you," she said, her voice even and precise, as cold as the winter winds in the concrete canyons of the city outside this club, and he would never know what that cost her. "Particularly by strange men renowned for their long years of compulsive promiscuity and generally loutish behavior."

He dropped his hand, but there was still that new light in his eyes, intense and certain, focused on her as if he saw all the things she'd hidden, her secrets and her scars. As if he knew she wore a mask. As if he could see it—and therefore, *her*—when no one else ever had.

That shook her, hard, but she fought to keep it from her face. Her eyes. Her rigid body that wanted things she'd never wanted, that she didn't know how to want.

"I'm renowned for other things, too," he pointed out, almost gently.

And she'd read about that, of course. His supposed sexual prowess. And she hated the fact that she could imagine it, too vividly now. Insistent. As if she was like other women, and could *yearn*—

Enough.

Zoe made a small noise that was too scornful to be laughter.

"Rich, bored men are remarkably predictable, Mr. Grant. I can assure you, I've seen every possible permutation of human perversity, and what has to be almost every last 'dungeon' on the island of Manhattan. Whips, chains, spanking benches, it's all so tiresome." She smiled, big and fake. "And though I'm sure your particular kinks are *fascinating,* I'll just take your word for it."

He laughed then, abruptly. And she didn't understand why she imagined she heard something there in that sound, something *more* and *deeper* than the tawdry, tedious legend of Hunter Grant, professional asshole. Something that suggested *he* was more than that when she knew, firsthand, that he wasn't.

He was the key to her revenge. That was all he was. And nothing else mattered. She wouldn't let it.

"There's only one way you're going to learn about my particular kinks," Hunter was saying, his voice shifting into something smoother, darker, connecting directly to that *thing* still too bright and too dangerous inside her, making her painfully aware that it was her own hunger. An impossible, alarming hunger for the very things she refused to let herself want. That she *didn't* want. He waited until she was looking at him again. "But you'll have to ask nicely."

She told herself she felt nothing then. No lick of fire. No kick of need.

Nothing, damn it. Not for a man like this.

"There is absolutely no chance of that ever happening." Her voice was flat. Cold.

He shook his head, though his blue eyes gleamed, and it was still like a shower of sparks inside her—and would terrify her, she was sure, if she let herself think about it.

"If you say so, Ms. Brook." But he smiled, confident and sure despite that darkness she sensed in him. Or maybe because of it. "Yet I find I'm suddenly much more interested in your…services."

It was time to remember who she was, who she'd become. What she'd been through. She wasn't sure why being near this man made her forget. She arched a brow.

"I don't ask nicely, Mr. Grant. I'm the one who's asked. And honestly? I prefer to be begged." She smiled then, the way he had. "You can start on your knees."

This time, he really did laugh, and yet he still didn't look anything but hungry as he regarded her from far too close, like some kind of ravenous wolf. Zoe couldn't remember the last time she'd felt like this. Daring, off-balance. Something other than in complete and total control.

When she knew perfectly well she would die before she'd let that happen. *Never, ever again.*

"I don't need any PR," he said, very softly, as if it was an endearment. "If that's really what you're offering."

She didn't know why she couldn't seem to pull in a full breath, why her eyes felt too bright, why the way he was looking at her then made her feel as if she was turned inside out. Exposed and vulnerable. How was that possible?

"It is."

"That's too bad." He was so big and entirely too beautiful, and she'd never been aware of another man the way she was of him—of every single part of him, especially that heated way he looked down at her. "Because if you wanted to see for yourself what the fuss was all about? Regarding my particular, predictable rich-man kinks? That, I could probably do."

It wasn't the first time a man had propositioned her. But it was the first time she'd felt a burst of flame lick over her when he did, and she was terribly afraid he knew that, too. That he felt the same slap of heat.

She couldn't let that happen, it was *impossible,* so she shoved it aside.

"Is that caveman code for 'sleep with me so I can put you

back in your proper place?"' she asked, cool and challenging and back on familiar ground, because she knew *this* routine. She could handle *this*. Jason Treffen had taught her well, one painful lesson at a time. "Because you should know before you try, dragging me off by my hair somewhere won't end the way you think it will. I can promise you that."

Hunter looked intrigued and his head canted slightly to one side, but that wolfish regard of his never wavered—bright and hot and *knowing*. Reaching much too far inside her, deep into her bones, like an ache.

It was that last part that made her wonder exactly how much control she was clinging to, after all.

"I don't want to drag you off somewhere by your hair and have my way with you, Ms. Brook."

The smile on her lips turned mocking, but she was more concerned with the sudden long, slow thump of her heart and the heavy, wet heat low in her belly. "Because you're not that kind of guy?"

There was something more than predatory in his eyes then, hard and hot, a dark knowing in the curve of his mouth that connected with that deep drumroll inside her, making it her pulse, her breath, her worst fear come true.

"I'm absolutely that kind of guy. But I told you. You have to ask me nicely."

He smiled, as if he was the one in control. And she couldn't allow it.

"No," she said, furious that it came out like a whisper,

thin and uncertain. His smile deepened for a moment, like a promise.

"Your loss," he murmured, and that aching fire swelled inside her, nearly bursting.

And then he laughed again, dismissing her that easily, and turned to go. *Again*. For good this time, she understood, and she couldn't let that happen.

Zoe had no choice.

"I wouldn't do that, Mr. Grant." She didn't know why that dryness in her mouth seemed to translate into something like trembling everywhere else, when she'd known before she'd approached him that it would probably come to this. She waited until he looked back at her, and pretended the blue gleam of his eyes didn't get to her at all, with all that weary amusement, as if he could see right through her when she knew—*she knew*—he couldn't. That no one could. She made herself smile. "I know about Sarah."

Chapter Two

Sarah.

That name seemed to echo through the club, drowning out the music, slamming everything else straight out of his head. It seared through Hunter's whole body like a lightning strike, only much darker. Much worse. Much more damaging.

He should have known.

If he hadn't been so thrown by the appearance of Zoe Brook—like a jolt of caffeine, dressed in slick dark colors that only emphasized the powerful punch of her smoky, blue-gray eyes and lips painted a dusky shade of red—he would have seen this coming, surely. She was wearing too many too-expensive clothes, for starters, which meant she wasn't flashing any skin. She hadn't thrown herself at him in lieu of a greeting. There was absolutely no reason at all she should get to him, much less make an entire club filled with far more conventionally beautiful and accessible women simply...fade.

And yet she'd been the only thing he could see, from the moment she'd locked eyes with him.

But women like Zoe didn't approach him at all these days, much less in places like this. They didn't seek him out. They thought they knew all they needed to know about him, and he went out of his way to confirm their low opinions. They condemned him from nice, safe distances, way up high on their moral high grounds, and he liked it that way. He didn't want to be near anyone he could ruin, not ever again.

He should have known.

Sarah was still the noose around his neck, all these years later. Forever. Deservedly—and he'd been kidding himself, thinking that he could avoid it now that he was back in New York. Imagining he could ignore the terrible truth. Blowing off his old friends' attempts to finally do something about what had happened to her, a decade too late.

"I beg your pardon?" He hardly sounded like himself, whoever the hell that was.

Zoe's smile affected him more than was healthy. Far more than was wise. "You heard me."

"Yes. But I don't think I know what you mean."

Her smile deepened, and he felt thrust off-balance. Angry and needy instead of his preferred state of numbness. Something like lost—and it was that last he found unforgivable. He'd accepted that he was the worst kind of man a decade ago. He'd proved it every day since, hadn't he? Why couldn't that be the end of it?

But it never was.

"Oh, I think you do," Zoe was saying almost cheerfully. "But you can pretend otherwise, if you like. I won't think less of you. I doubt that's even possible. Either way, I'll expect you at my office tomorrow morning at ten."

"Your expectations are destined to end in disappointment."

"I hope not." Her perfectly wicked brows rose, and he didn't know what was the matter with him, that she could threaten him and he wanted her anyway. "I'm very good at getting what I want, Mr. Grant. You don't want to test me."

"Are you blackmailing me, Ms. Brook?"

Her smoke-colored eyes filled with a gleaming sort of triumph, making her look nearly beautiful in the club's dark light. But Hunter had made beautiful women his life's work, and Zoe Brook didn't fit the bill. She was too sharp, too edgy. Her full lips were too quick to a smirk and her cool, blue-gray gaze was far too direct and intelligent. Her dark hair was thick and inky, her figure trim and smooth beneath clothes that murmured of her success in elegant lines, but she wasn't anything as palatable as *pretty.* He liked softness and sweetness. Obliging whispers, melting glances. She was too…*much*.

And that was without knowing that when he touched her, he caught fire.

"That would suggest that there's something about your ex-girlfriend that could be used to blackmail you," she said after a moment of consideration. Her mouth twitched. "Are you saying there is?"

"I have no idea. I don't know what you're talking about." Hunter smiled. "But then, everyone knows what a dumb jock I am."

"I don't think you're dumb," she said, and not in a complimentary way. "Whatever else you are."

"You may be right," he agreed, amused. "It takes a certain level of intelligence to remain this committed to my own destruction." He held her gaze. "But that still doesn't mean I know what you're talking about."

There was a small pause, and the world crept back in. The insistent pulse of the club's loud music. The distant sound of laughter. His own heart, pounding hard.

"You're remarkably self-aware for a Neanderthal, I have to admit," she said then, as if she was extending an olive branch.

"I was a Neanderthal professionally, never socially. It's a crucial distinction."

"Are you telling me you're the way you are *deliberately?*"

"Aren't we all?" he asked, more harshly than he'd intended. Giving too much away, he saw, when she tilted her head slightly to one side and regarded him with uncomfortable frankness.

He needed to walk away from this woman. He needed to end this conversation. He didn't know why he couldn't seem to do it. Why he stood there before her as if waiting for her to render judgment—when he knew she already had. Before she'd arrived, no doubt, or she wouldn't have sought him out like this.

When it shouldn't matter anyway.

"I'd be very careful playing this game, if I were you," he said quietly. Too quietly. Showing more than he should, again. "You might not like where it goes."

"Don't worry," she said, something so sharp in her gaze it looked like hatred, and that shouldn't have surprised him. Not anymore. It certainly shouldn't have made him feel so hollowed out, as if she'd done it herself with a jagged spoon while they stood here like this, close enough to touch. "I'm not going to hurt myself because you're mean to me, Mr. Grant. I'm not her."

It was a shot through the heart. Unerring and lethal.

Zoe Brook smiled again, wider than before.

"Ten o'clock," she told him while he stood there like a dead thing, as he was certain she'd intended. Her amused drawl in place and that cool fire in her eyes that reminded him of the sea outside his family's rambling cottage high on the Maine coast, where he'd seen this precise shade of dangerous gray at Christmas. And that rawness in him that grew the more she looked at him and saw nothing but the dark and terrible things he'd done.

Hunter preferred himself empty. At least then he knew who he was.

She reached over and pressed a business card into his hand. "Don't be late."

And when she walked away, he stayed where she left him, as surely as if she'd cut him off at the knees.

As if there was nothing left of him but shattered pieces. Shadows and lies where his bones should have been. Ruins of the man he'd never been.

This is the *life you made,* he told himself when he finally pushed his way out of the club into the cold, crisp February morning some time later, the slap of winter harsh against his face.

Hunter hailed a cab out on the frigid avenue and then stared out the window as Manhattan slid by on the jerky trip back toward his soulless, minimalist penthouse that towered above Wall Street: the perfect crypt for the walking dead, he'd thought when he'd bought it a few months back.

After all, he'd been the one to punch that smug referee in the face in December in the middle of a hotly contested call; he'd known what he was doing and he'd known what was likely to happen when he did it. He simply hadn't cared enough any longer to bother restraining himself. His whole career had been an exercise in pushing limits. He'd been benched, fined, reprimanded. He'd once told a reporter that he wanted to see what it took to be ejected from the NFL altogether—and as he'd finally proved, he hadn't been joking.

"And behold," he'd told two of his three college roommates with his typical self-aggrandizing swagger at their depressing annual dinner, before their odd vigil had become even more upsetting than it usually was with an anonymous letter and a host of unsavory accusations he didn't want to think about.

He'd shown off his scraped knuckles with the pretense of great pride, fooling neither of the men who had once known him so well, but that was how they'd rolled for years. Big smiles. Great stories. A howling abyss within.

Or maybe that was him.

"I am a success in all I do," he'd said, grinning widely at Austin Treffen and Alex Diaz as if they were all still eighteen years old and bursting with hopes and dreams and grand ideas about what their lives would be. Instead of what they actually were. What they'd let themselves become in these years of silence. *Bought and paid for. Complicit.* "As ever."

But he didn't want to think about Sarah Michaels, especially now that Zoe Brook had thrown her in his face. He'd been avoiding it since the night she'd died, but fate and that damned letter Austin had slapped down on the table that night in December had intervened.

Ten years ago, Hunter had suspected that Sarah had betrayed him after their three intense years of dating, from college into their first year of life in New York City. *That,* he'd thought, was why she'd broken up with him back then. He'd believed guilt over her behavior had led her to take her own life that awful night, and he'd never forgiven himself for his role in her decision. That he'd been terribly wrong about her had been clear after she'd died, and that had been bad enough. But the letter Austin had received had suggested it was so much worse than that—so much *more*—

Hunter didn't see how he could live with what he knew now. With himself, for not knowing it then.

He was a heartless, soulless man, he knew: blind and self-ish to the core. He'd wasted his life as if he'd been on a mission to do so from the start. He'd disappointed his family, his friends, both football teams he'd played for in his career, all of his fans. He'd squandered each and every gift he'd ever been given. He'd let the only girl he'd ever loved walk away from him, straight into the hands of a monster, and he hadn't noticed anything but his own pain and jealousy.

And he knew these were the least of his sins.

Because he still remembered every moment of that night ten years ago, at the annual Christmas party at Austin's father's law firm. How Sarah had come to him with all that dark pain on her face and he had *liked* it.

Can I talk to you? she'd asked. *Please?*

Maybe later, he'd said, making such a show of not caring, of hardly paying attention to her. *This is a big night.*

It was about time she'd felt some of what he was feeling, he'd thought. He'd *liked* that she looked lost and scared and tentative, all things Sarah Michaels had never been. He'd assumed that she was finally recognizing what a huge mistake she'd made in breaking up with him. He'd thought it was so ironic that he'd been entirely faithful to Sarah even though he was the professional athlete—that she'd been the one to cheat on him, and with Austin's *father,* no less.

He'd been so smugly certain he was the victim. So self-righteous that Sarah had done this terrible thing and he—out of respect for who she'd been back in college, he'd told himself piously—had opted to keep it to himself. Because he was such a great guy.

And because he was all things petty, because he'd thought that shattered look on her face—all about him, he'd been so certain—wasn't *quite* enough, he'd taken the whole thing a step further and asked the bimbo he'd been parading around on his arm to marry him, right there in the middle of the Christmas party in all of the elegance and old-money sparkle Treffen, Smith, and Howell claimed as its own.

He'd watched Sarah leave the room as the champagne was popped, looking small and beaten, and all these years later he was still ashamed of how deeply satisfied he'd felt then. He'd had no idea that that would be the last time he'd ever see her. That he'd spend the rest of his life wondering if, had he known he'd never lay eyes on Sarah alive again, he might have done something differently.

One shade up from sociopathic, Zoe Brook had said. She had no idea how right she was.

Then again, if she knew about Sarah, maybe she did.

Zoe didn't take a full breath until she shut her apartment door late that night, cutting herself off from the world at last. She tugged off her boots in her entry hall and padded barefoot into the apartment that ambled over the whole of the third floor of a prewar brownstone on the Upper West Side.

She let herself breathe in deep as she moved through the living room with its commotion of bright colors, letting her Tough Bitch Mask drop away. Here at home, she was someone else. Here, she was the Zoe she might have been.

The Zoe who hadn't been ruined.

She moved into her bathroom as she stripped out of her work clothes, headed for the pretty claw-footed tub perched on the black-and-white checkerboard tiled floor. She turned on the water and poured in a sachet of her favorite bath salts, letting the lavender scent work on her.

There was more Jason Treffen in her head than usual tonight, and it made her edgy.

Her interaction with Hunter Grant this morning hadn't helped. The thing was, she'd wanted to touch him again, standing there in the middle of a *strip club,* of all places. She'd wanted to *touch* him, and that didn't make sense. Not for her.

Her skin felt itchy. New. As if it wasn't hers any longer. And that strange notion threw her right back into the past.

Her grandparents had raised her grudgingly after her own parents took off, reminding her daily that they were doing no more than their Christian duty. And that was exactly what they'd done. She'd grown up in the high desert of southern California, whole worlds and a long drive away from glamorous Los Angeles. It had been bitterly cold in the winter, brutally hot in the summer, and there was always that unsettling desert wind, sweeping down from the stark, brown mountains to keep everyone on edge.

Zoe had tried her best to love her grandparents and their

pinched-mouthed charity they'd never allowed her to forget would end the day she turned eighteen. She'd tried. School hadn't come easily to her, but she'd applied herself and excelled her way into a scholarship—because she'd had no other choice if she wanted to escape.

When she met Jason Treffen at a scholarship student function her senior year at Cornell, he was charming and kind. He *understood*. And because he did, when he offered to help her, she let him.

She still couldn't forgive herself for that.

He'd paid off her student loans because, he said, he knew promise when he saw it. He'd hired her as a legal assistant at his very upscale law firm in New York City, and Zoe had been so grateful. For the first time in her life, she'd felt cared for. Pampered, even. As if she'd been worthy of love after all, despite her grandparents.

It wasn't until the second time Jason asked her to go out to dinner with a friend of his—because the old guy was lonely and Zoe was a pretty girl who could be friendly, couldn't she?—that she got that sick feeling in her gut. It wasn't until one or two more "favors" ended with increasingly intense negotiations for sex that Jason suggested later she should have accepted, that she finally understood. That she finally saw the wolf in his gleaming sheep's robes.

But by then, of course, she was trapped. Jason was good at what he did. And even better at punishing the girls who didn't play along. He was rich and powerful and connected, and, as he told her repeatedly, no one would believe her anyway.

It took Zoe three long, horrible years to buy her freedom. She watched other girls give in. To drugs, to despair. She almost wavered herself—it was so hard, and she was so alone, and did she really think she could beat a powerful man such as Jason at his own game?—but then her friend Sarah had taken her own life.

And that had changed everything.

Zoe had understood she had to escape. *She had to.* Or all of it—Sarah's death, what she'd suffered those terrible years, what had happened to the other girls—would have been in vain.

She had to escape, or Jason won.

Zoe twisted her long black hair into a messy knot on the top of her head now, and tested the water in the bath, letting it run through her fingers. And it all rushed back. It flooded into her, demanding her surrender, the way it always did.

Insisting she remember everything.

Do you really believe you can run away from me? Jason had laughed at her that last day in his dark wood office so high above the city, when she'd thrown her hard-earned check down in front of him and told him she was done. Leaving. Free at last. *I plucked you from obscurity. You don't have anything I didn't give you, and you never will. Remember that.*

You made me a whore, she'd thrown at him, hatred and terror and disgust making her voice too thick. Too obvious.

Whores generally close the deal. He'd looked so pleased with himself. So smug. Not in the least bit concerned that she was getting out from under his thumb. *That's the point of whores. What you do is play dangerous games. You're lucky there are so many men who enjoy paying for the privilege of that kind of tease.*

But she'd had one or two nights that had tipped over that edge, hadn't she? When they'd simply taken what they wanted. And the way he'd looked at her then, she knew that he knew it.

Yes, she'd hissed at him. *Lucky is exactly how I feel. I'm overcome with gratitude.*

You will be, he'd assured her.

Years had passed and she still couldn't get the ring of his laughter out of her ears, erase that vicious smile from her memory.

Hello, Zoe.

He'd surprised her backstage in the green room of one of the nighttime shows that taped locally that time, where she'd been shepherding a client as part of her first job in PR. She'd stared at him, hoping he'd disappear the way he sometimes did in the nightmares she'd refused to admit she'd been having since her escape from Treffen, Smith, and Howell.

But, of course, he'd only smiled at her.

It wouldn't kill you to be polite, he'd said, kindly, but she could see the monster in his eyes.

In fact, she'd said, *it might.*

His smile had only deepened, turned friendlier. Jason Treffen at his most dangerous.

Enjoy that sassy spirit of yours, he'd said, as if he'd been bestowing a gift upon her. *It won't last.*

Some of her coworkers had burst into the room then and had been wowed at the sight of Jason Treffen, saint of New York, standing there with a lowly new PR associate like Zoe. She'd had to smile politely while he took pictures with them. When he'd slung an arm around her shoulders. While he'd chatted with them, doling out his usual host of platitudes and insights, all of which took on a nightmarish hue should you happen to know what lurked beneath it.

He'd engineered that meeting, she knew he had. To remind her that whenever he so desired, he could reach out and make her feel slimy and cheap. Used.

Zoe had already vowed she'd take him down some day. After that run-in, she'd determined that she wanted it to *hurt.* And her desire for revenge had burned in her, a naked flame, hot and bright. Eclipsing everything else.

You exist because I allow it, he'd told her at a charity event not five years ago, cupping her elbow in his hand and making her feel as if a thousand insects swarmed over her skin. *Everything you own, all you've accomplished, is mine. I gave it to you and I can take it away, Zoe.*

She hadn't been quite so young then. And she hadn't much cared that she was dead inside.

I can't imagine why you'd bother, she'd said, and she'd been so proud that she'd stood there as if turned to stone, as if it didn't matter that he was touching her.

Why do I do anything? Again, that nasty laugh. He'd dug

his fingers into the tender place above her elbow, making her whole arm numb. She'd remembered that he'd liked pain. Inflicting it, watching others suffer it. But she'd only stared back at him, cool and unimpressed, unwilling to give him the satisfaction of reacting. *Because I can, Zoe. I can do whatever the hell I want. Remember that.*

The last time she'd seen him had been some months ago. She'd been in a very fancy restaurant celebrating the birthday of one of her former clients, who also happened to be a heavyweight in New York politics. She'd expected to see Jason there, working the party in his usual way, and she hadn't been disappointed.

She'd braced herself for the inevitable encounter—but he hadn't approached her. He'd been reveling in a crowd of admirers until a young woman appeared at his side and whispered something in his ear.

Zoe had seen the way Jason let his hand rest a moment too long on the young woman's arm. She'd seen the way he'd turned to look down at her, seen the flash of that repulsive smile of his that had made her stomach lurch from all the way across the room. She'd seen them turn toward the door, the woman stepping out to walk in front of him, so he couldn't see her face any longer.

That face which had been a blank except for her eyes, which were dark with self-loathing and sheer, stark misery.

Zoe knew that expression. *She knew.* It had been like a kick to the gut, so hard she hadn't been able to breathe, and she'd had to stand still and *watch.*

Then she'd felt something else—that creeping, sickening feeling that told her he'd seen her. Sure enough, when she'd jerked her gaze away from the young woman who hurried from the party and out into the fall night, Jason was watching her.

He'd held her gaze across the crowd. So arrogant. So superior. She'd clenched her fingers so hard around the stem of her wineglass that she'd left deep grooves in her own flesh. She'd worried that she might be sick where she stood.

Jason Treffen had merely smiled. Pleased, as ever. Winning, as usual.

Zoe sucked in a breath now, snapping herself back into her own bathroom. *You're safe,* she told herself, again and again, until her heart rate smoothed out. She stepped into the hot water, and sank into its silken embrace until she was submerged up to her chin.

At last, it was time. The whole country was gearing up to celebrate Jason Treffen and his many years of humanitarian "service" to all, and that was where Zoe came in. It was time to take him down. It was time to hit him where it hurt. Past time.

It was time to do some winning of her own.

And Hunter Grant—who had dated Sarah Michaels back when Zoe and Sarah were both caught in Jason's trap, who had broken that poor girl's heart, who had flaunted another woman in Sarah's face on the night she'd died, and that was assuming he hadn't been doing something far worse—was going to help her do it.

Or Zoe would destroy him, too.

No matter how he made her feel.

Hunter hated Midtown with a passion.

He hated the streets crammed full of grim worker drones, so self-important and brusque. He hated the building that housed Treffen, Smith, and Howell, an architecturally uninspired black box indistinguishable from the rest of the block it stood on. He hated the press of the crowds on the streets outside. The ubiquitous hot dog vendors, the stink of the subways that rose up through the grates at his feet, the black sparkle of the listless fountain that dominated the courtyard entryway to the building and stood waterless this time of year, like a metaphor.

He hadn't set foot in this building since the night of that terrible Christmas party ten years ago.

But he was under siege from at least three different lawsuits these days thanks to his antics, and so he'd finally agreed to meet his legal team today in this hateful place. This grand, gluttonous monument to so many lies.

Hunter knew he could very well run into Jason here. And probably would. The man's name was etched into the wall, after all. He didn't know what he'd do if that happened.

He knew what he *wanted* to do, what he should have done ten years ago: punch the smug, insufferable bastard in the face, which was only the smallest part of what Jason Treffen deserved.

Maybe it was time to make sure he got it—but, of course, that would require *action*.

Austin had spent the time since their ghoulish little December anniversary dinner exposing his father for the monster he was to his family. Alex had spent it plotting out ways to further make Jason pay, publicly. Austin and Alex *had plans*. They wanted to take Jason down and they had *ideas* about how to do it. Austin had already done his part. Alex was working on his.

While Hunter was avoiding the entire thing, as if that might make it go away. Along with most of the texts and calls he received from his old friends, while he was at it.

He didn't bother scowling at his reflection in the gleaming elevator doors before him as he rocketed up toward the firm. He knew what was looking back at him. If anything, Zoe Brook had been too conservative in her rundown of his flaws.

The doors slid open, and Hunter wasn't at all surprised to see a young woman standing there, looking sleek and polished and delighted to see him.

Looking like déjà vu.

"Hello, Mr. Grant," she said, smiling. "I'm Iris."

If he had to guess, he'd say she was the latest incarnation of what Sarah had been. The title had been *Legal Assistant* back then. But if this one was another of Jason's girls, doing paralegal work was the very tip of the iceberg.

And that twisting, nasty feeling in his gut told him he

knew exactly what that iceberg entailed, and that this girl was part of it. Up to her neck and drowning, no doubt.

One more victim he couldn't save. How many were there now? How many more would there be before he actually did something about it? How many people could say their blind inaction had an actual body count?

"Nice to meet you, Iris," he said, and he could hear the gravel in his voice. That banked fury, as toothless as the rest of him. He forced a smile. "Are you here to make sure I don't get lost?"

"Mr. Treffen sent me to collect you," Iris said. "He wanted you to drop in and say hello before your meeting."

If she noticed the way Hunter froze, or the way his smile vanished from his face, she was too well trained to comment on it. And God help him, he didn't want to think about Jason fucking Treffen's *training program*.

"It's this way," she said.

But he didn't follow her when she started to move. He stood there by the bank of elevators, wishing he was a different man.

"Mr. Grant?"

"Please tell Mr. Treffen I don't have time to see him today," Hunter said, his voice clipped. *Because I don't know if I'll try to kill him with my bare hands. Or if I should try to stop myself if I do. Or if—even worse—I'll do nothing at all.* "I'm sure he'll understand."

Iris's polite mask never altered. "Of course," she said smoothly.

And Hunter let her walk away, straight back into hell,

the way he'd let Sarah ten years ago. He even told himself it was better that way.

Because he made every single thing he touched that much worse.

That evening, Austin escalated to all-caps texts.

Having avoided one Treffen today, Hunter thought he'd do well to avoid the other, too. Not that it was fair, precisely, to lump the two together.

Good thing Hunter didn't care.

The winter night had slammed down outside, dark and frigid and uninviting. It wasn't much better inside his mausoleum of a penthouse, which seemed to loom all around him tonight, swollen black and thick with all his sins. He sat in the dark, watching *SportsCenter* on his laughably huge television that took up the better part of one vast wall.

He blew out a breath when Jason Treffen appeared onscreen, remembering that this was one of the reasons his old friends were so motivated to act. Now, when Jason was a few weeks away from being celebrated on national television, and every other advertisement seemed to trumpet his smiling face, as if he was running for office. Unopposed. The coverage was relentless.

Treffen, tireless advocate for women, in his first and most indepth interview!

Treffen, defender of the downtrodden and personal benefactor to so many, opens up at last!

It was almost a relief when the regular programming returned, and one of Hunter's former teammates—who happened to be suing him—appeared on the screen. Hunter muted him, not wanting to hear, yet again, a rundown of the ways in which his ejection from the NFL was a blessing for all concerned.

But, "He's never been a team player," he could see his former wide receiver say, directly into the camera, as if he knew Hunter was watching him, sound off or not. This was all part of the same song and dance that every single person in pro football had been performing since mid-December, whether they were filing lawsuits against him or not. Hunter could recite it himself, nearly word for word.

Out for himself. Not a team player. Prima donna. Waste of potential, waste of resources, narcissistic—

Blah-blah-blah.

It seemed like the perfect time, then, to call an old friend he didn't want to talk to, to discuss a subject he still didn't want to think about.

I know about Sarah, Zoe Brook had said. Which meant he hadn't stopped thinking about it, no matter how little he wanted that.

"Stop texting me." Hunter grunted into his cell phone when Austin answered—profanely, as expected. "You're like a fourteen-year-old girl. I'm busy."

"Busy doing what, playing hard to get?" Austin let out a short laugh. "Because last I checked, you don't have a job."

"I have shit to do. Didn't realize I had to clear my schedule through a social secretary."

"You're sitting in your lonely bachelor pad, all by your-self, weeping over your glory days on ESPN On Demand," Austin said disparagingly. "Aren't you?"

Ouch. "I'll repeat—stop texting me. When I'm tired of my glory days, you'll be the first to know."

"News flash, douchebag, this isn't even about you. It was never about you."

"Then you have even less reason to harass me."

"Of course your reaction is to disappear." Austin sounded exasperated. "Why am I surprised? Why did I think this time would be any different?"

"Because you're such a giddy optimist?"

"This is what you do," Austin said, as if he hadn't heard Hunter's sarcasm. "You did it ten years ago, you're doing it now."

"This conversation is reminding me why I don't do girl-friends. Should we talk about where our relationship is heading? Do you feel fat? Are you going to tell me about your hurt feelings next?"

"I think you exhibited your feelings all over the foot-ball field, and the tabloids, for the past ten years," Austin retorted. "All while keeping as far away from this cesspool as you could."

Hunter didn't say anything, because it was true. After Sarah's death, he'd bailed. He'd moved out of the apartment he'd shared with Austin and Alex in New York, without a word. He'd gotten himself transferred to Dallas by the start of the next season, and he'd never had any intention of coming back to New York. Or to these old friendships that had once been more important to him than his own family.

"Do you have something in particular you wanted to talk about, Austin?" he asked now, scrubbing his face with one hand. "Or did you just want to reach out and sweet talk me? I appreciate it, I do, but next time, no need to call. Flowers would be fine. Don't really like roses, though."

"Is this what happens to you if you're not playing football? Stop talking about flowers."

"Tulips would do. I also like stargazer lilies. And the occasional hydrangea."

He had no idea what he was talking about. But he was also smirking into the darkness all around him, which felt like an improvement. It reminded him of those long-ago days when he would have called Austin a brother.

"Did you get hit on the head today?" Austin asked. "Harder than usual, I mean?"

It only made Hunter want to talk about, say, shrubbery. Lawn ornaments. The little-known joys of vegetable gardens. He restrained himself, barely.

"I get it," Austin said with a familiar edge in his voice, when moments ticked by and Hunter remained silent. He'd sounded much the same the last time Hunter had seen him, in some swanky bar or another, where Hunter had pretended he was the kind of man who cared about… anything. "This is the part where you hide in plain sight, right? Pretend you're not involved? Just like you did back then?"

"I don't know what you're talking about," Hunter lied, and it was impossible to imagine he'd been making jokes about flowers only moments before. As if he and Austin were still close. He needed to remember that he'd lost everything the night they'd lost Sarah. Every single thing he'd ever thought was important. "I'm right here. Having this phone call, when usually, that number of stalkery texts leads straight to a court order."

"I don't know why I'm surprised. Is there anyone in your life you haven't let down, Hunter? Anyone at all?"

He thought of his deeply appalled parents, who had never understood his desire to play football, much less his penchant for public scandals involving his notably bad temper and far worse decisions. His brother JP, the mogul in the making, who only shook his head at Hunter's antics, but certainly didn't depend on Hunter for anything. Even his younger sister, Nora, who had once looked at him with all that hero worship in her eyes, had spent all of their traditional Grant family Christmas up in Maine sighing heavily every time she'd found herself alone with him. As if his expulsion from football had finally forced even her to see him the way everyone else did.

"You should have sent a bouquet, Austin," Hunter said now. "Much less drama and disappointment all around."

Later, he sat in the dark, with only the television for company, and told himself he liked it that way.

He was thirty-three years old and he'd alienated every single person who'd ever meant something to him. Some men earned their lives of quiet desperation, their solitary confinement. An empty house, an abandoned life, another long winter all alone.

Zoe Brook was kidding herself: there was no rehabilitating him. There was no point pretending.

Hunter had never been destined for anything but this.

Chapter Three

"Is this why you missed another appointment, Mr. Grant, or is this just a little bit of wallowing on a weekday night? Self-indulgence, perhaps? I hate to mention it, but it *looks* like self-pity."

For a moment, Hunter thought he was dreaming that sharp, amused voice that could belong to only one person. But he wasn't asleep. He'd driven himself crazy on his couch for a while after speaking to Austin, and had then taken himself off to his extraordinarily expensive health club to sweat it out on the treadmill. Mile after brutal mile, until his legs felt shaky and weak. And then he'd sat in the whirlpool tub with the jets on high, pretending his mind was perfectly fucking clear.

Zoe Brook stood there when he opened his eyes, much like one of the many apparitions he hadn't been thinking about. She wore another impressively sleek dress today, this one in a gunmetal gray that skimmed over her lean curves and made his mouth go dry, with a long and complicated sweater over it. Her lips were red, her eyes were cool, and there was no reason at all she should be looking at him like that at eleven o'clock at night.

"I think this confirms that you're stalking me," he said, instead of all the other things he wanted to say. "Do I need to call security?"

"This isn't stalking. This is persistence. I can understand why you'd be unfamiliar with the concept."

"Tomayto, tomahto," he murmured.

She smiled that wicked smile of hers, and he was glad the bubbles concealed the most unruly part of him from view. He stretched his arms out along the sides of the hot tub and smiled back.

Suddenly, he was wide awake. Clearheaded, even. At last. More focused than he'd been in years.

"I know you couldn't possibly have missed your appointment today *on purpose,*" she said, in a bright and easy way at complete odds with the shrewd look she was giving him. "But I'm afraid that's two strikes."

"I don't respond well to baseball metaphors. It's a football thing. Jets, Sharks. You know how it is."

"Let's try it again, shall we? Ten o'clock on Thursday. Don't make me come after you again."

"Or what?" he asked drily. "We'll *both* get naked and wet?"

A group of women walked by then, chatting idly while wrapped in towels from the locker room and completely unaware that they were interrupting something electric. Their conversation cut off abruptly when they saw Hunter lounging in the hot tub, then exploded into a frenzy of giggles when he smiled at them.

They giggled louder, then disappeared into the sauna, where there was a sudden burst of high-pitched squealing as the door swung closed.

"I think they recognized me," he said.

"Well," Zoe said, in that prickly way of hers that made him grin. "You're certainly recognizable."

He stood then, stretching his arms over his head and letting the hot water course over him, entirely too amused by the way her eyes widened at the sight of his naked torso, then dropped to the board shorts that were plastered to his thighs. He *felt* the way she swallowed, hard. Her blue-gray eyes traced over his skin, in a manner he was sure left fingerprints behind.

He wanted her even more than he remembered he had in that strip club, where she'd stood out like a beacon and made him forget himself. He wanted to taste the elegant line of her neck, see what lay beneath those beautiful clothes. He wanted to see where that flush in her cheeks led, if it moved over the rest of her smooth skin and turned it that pretty blush color.

God, the ways he wanted her. Here, now. Anywhere.

"Why don't we have this meeting of yours right now?" he asked, watching her narrowly. Willing her to close the distance between them, so he could touch her again. Feel that fire. She made him imagine he was alive again, and as much as he disliked what came along with that, he still found he liked the burn. "You've gone to the trouble to track me down in my gym in the middle of the night. You have my full attention."

But there were ghosts in her eyes when she dragged them back to his.

"Not yet," she said softly. Deliberately. "But I will. Ten o'clock on Thursday, Mr. Grant."

"Will I hear about this plan of yours?" he asked, somewhere between dry and amused, and his body didn't care which, it just wanted her. Particularly when she let out that laugh. "Or will you continue to drop vague hints and not-so-veiled threats?"

"Keep your appointment," she suggested.

"I like your style," he said, swinging his leg over the side of the tub and climbing out, watching her eyes widen slightly before she controlled it. "Intrigue and drama over an appointment I didn't make and don't want. I appreciate the effort, Ms. Brook. I do."

"Just think how appreciative you'll be on Thursday," she said with a smile that made him think of sweet cream and oversatisfied cats.

Hunter picked up his towel and swiped it over his face, and when he lowered it, she was gone. That shouldn't have surprised him. Or made him laugh enough to hear the echo of it from the tile around him, reminding him of a man he barely recognized that had once been him.

He got dressed quickly in the locker room, and then he started making some calls. He might have been a pariah, but that didn't mean he was any less famous. People still took his calls—even in the middle of the night.

Zoe Brook was the best, he found—just as she'd claimed. She could solve any image problem, make any kind of piggish behavior into a festival of silk purses, all without seeming to break a sweat. She was the real deal.

"The only trouble," Zair al Ruyi, his friend and the fourth roommate from their early Harvard days, told him from Washington, D.C., where he was currently serving as ambassador to the United States from his far-off, oil-rich sultanate, "is that she might very well chew you up and spit you out while she's saving you from the jaws of the lion. It's her specialty."

"Luckily," Hunter said, "I make a pretty thin meal. Not much left to chew on."

Zair, keeper of his own dark secrets and certainly no stranger to trouble, diplomatic immunity or no, laughed.

"She can solve any problem. Even one of yours."

"And you know this from personal experience?" Hunter asked, cradling his phone between his head and his shoulder as he walked out into the cold night. "Please tell me that for the first time in our entire history, you plan to share."

If there was anyone cagier or more private than Zair, Hunter had never met him. They'd been sophomores before Hunter had realized that when Zair made vague references to "home," he'd meant a sultan's palace. Or when he'd said "my brother," he'd meant *the Sultan of Ruyi.*

His old friend only laughed now, making Hunter wish

things were different. That instead of chasing footballs across the past decade, he'd made more of an effort to stay connected to these first, best friends of his, more like brothers than his own, actual brother had ever been. But he'd lost that, too.

"Whatever Zoe Brook wants with you, Hunter," Zair said, not answering the question directly, not that Hunter would have known what to do if he had, "I'd give it to her. Because otherwise I suspect she'll simply go ahead and take it."

He met Zoe in the waiting room of her bold Columbus Circle office at precisely ten-fifteen on Thursday morning. Hunter lounged on one of the bright red leather couches as if he were in his own living room, a detail he saw her take in with a single amused glance. Her wicked brows rose at once, and he felt it like a blast of heat dancing all over his skin. Like the brush of her fingers against his sex.

"Look at that." She sounded faintly mocking. "You *can* find your way across the city. And all by yourself!"

"Third time's the charm," he agreed in the same tone, aware that the receptionist was staring at him in something like awe. Or was it horror? "You could say I had a change of heart in the gym the other night."

"Men your age need to be careful," she said as if agreeing, and he had to grin at the slap of it. Especially since he knew perfectly well she was all of a year younger than he was. "Your hearts aren't what they were when you were young."

"I was visited by an apparition of annoying conversations past," he said mildly. "She irritated me into coming here. It was that or sink into a coma of indifference."

Zoe smiled, slow and triumphant, and that was even hotter. It made him wish they were alone. It made him care less by the second about the fact they weren't.

"A coma might have been something of an improvement, Mr. Grant, all things considered," she said, as if she could read his dirty mind. He hoped she could. He'd spent a significant amount of time imagining a different and far more satisfying ending to that hot tub encounter over the past few days. "Why don't you follow me?"

Hunter lost himself in the sway of her hips in that delectable skirt she wore as she turned and he followed. The sweet curve of her bottom. The way she walked—that confident swagger that made his whole body tighten—in those lickable shoes with the clever red soles that peeked at him with every step, like an invitation to the best kind of sin.

He accepted. Happily.

"You say you're good at what you do," Hunter said as she led him down the bright, airy hall toward her private office.

"I don't have to say it." That razor-sharp curve of her lips, thrown over her shoulder, was the best thing he'd seen in years. It made even those great, dark spaces in him seem to sing with light. With heat. "My work speaks for itself, and usually on the nightly news. Or when I'm really good? Not at all. No news cycles. No whispers. Not even a speculative paragraph in the fringe tabloids, stuck in between UFO sightings. I make it disappear completely, as if it never happened at all."

"Like magic."

"Something like that. Just more expensive."

"I enjoyed that character assassination you treated me to in the strip club the other day," Hunter drawled. "Is that how it usually works? Break the clients down into bite-size pieces so they'll be grateful when you put them back together into your preferred image, whatever that might be?"

"Don't look behind the curtain, Mr. Grant," she said, without looking at him this time, her voice filled with the laughter he couldn't see. But he wanted to see it. He wanted to bathe in it. Again and again, as if it could finally wash him clean. "Just accept the wave of the PR wand. It's as magical as you let it be."

"I've been on a few sports teams, Ms. Brook. I know you have to tear me down to build me back up. It's Psychological Warfare 101."

"Then I expect you'll be the model client, won't you?"

She waved him into her office and closed the door behind them. He looked around as she walked toward her desk, taking in the crispness of the white walls, the cold concrete floors with scattered area rugs in muted colors to cushion the chill. The frigidity was relieved only by the view of the city out her windows and the typical vanity wall of photographs featuring Zoe with various famous and/or powerful people. Happy clients, presumably.

He recognized most of them, and noted that Zair was in

the top left, his usual too-handsome, too-serious self, his unsmiling face on this particular wall another mystery that would likely never be solved. Her desk was scrupulously neat, made entirely of heavy sheets of metal and glass, and he suspected she knew exactly how formidable and untouchable she looked when she rested against the front of it, leaning back to regard him coolly.

Trouble was, he didn't respond to messages like that the way he should. The way he was no doubt intended to respond. He wanted to…mess her up a little. Make all of that chilly control bleed into something else, something at least as hot and as wild and as deeply foolish as the thing that hummed in him, demanding he go over there and lose his hands in that slick twist of her hair, take her wicked, argumentative mouth with his, pull those impossibly long legs around his waist and sink into her with those sexy red-soled shoes still on her feet.

He wanted to know why she was targeting him, what she was after.

What she thought she knew about Sarah.

So he kept walking, over the cold floor that made his boots sound like drums, past the sitting area that was set up off to the right and was no doubt where she meant for him to go, to a low sofa that would put him at her knees.

He didn't think so.

He moved closer and closer, watching the way she fought to keep from reacting, the way her fascinating face tightened and then smoothed out almost in the same instant, as if she'd had to order herself to stay so calm. He certainly hoped she did.

And then he was looming over her. Wholly and unapologetically and inappropriately in her space. As if, should he crook his head just slightly, he might finally taste that smart mouth of hers. It would be that easy.

She tilted her chin up to keep holding his gaze, but otherwise, showed him nothing but that cool wariness she wore like a shield. He wondered what it cost her.

He didn't know why he wanted to know, as if it was a desperate thing inside him, clawing its way out.

"Perhaps," she said, and though her voice was mild he could hear a darkness beneath it. A hint of something raw that shouldn't have called to him, sung in him. "I should have been slightly more clear about what I meant by *model client*."

"Tell me why you came after me," he said. "What you want."

There was nothing but a scant breath of space between their bodies, and he'd have bet his entire fortune that she wanted to stand up straight to regain a little bit of height, and her edge. But didn't, because he'd know exactly why she was doing it. He imagined that was also the reason she didn't tell him to back off. It would be too revealing.

He smiled. He'd always been good at games like this. "Tell me, and I'll behave."

"Is this an example of you behaving, Mr. Grant?" Her

voice was light. Airy. Her gaze was not. "Because it feels a bit more like a crude attempt at intimidation."

"Not at all. I'm never crude."

The problem was, this close, he found it hard to concentrate on things like strategy. He could smell the faintest hint of lavender on her skin, and wanted to follow it. Taste it. Strip away her clothes and feast on the flesh beneath until they were both in pieces. On her desk, on the floor, wherever.

He dropped his gaze to her mouth, which was fuller and more tempting this close. Like a beacon it hurt him to ignore. "This is the first step toward a bright and shiny new me. Just tell me what you want with me."

"Rehabilitation isn't easy for anyone," she said, her voice a little bit *too* even. He felt it like a victory, adrenaline and need coursing through him, drumming louder than his boots had against the hard floor. "It depends on the client, and clients tend to have difficulty with the most crucial part of it." She waited until he dragged his gaze back up to hers, and held it for a beat or two. "For starters, you have to do what I say."

"What happens to clients who don't?"

"They all do, eventually."

"No one is entirely successful, Ms. Brook," he pointed out, his voice lower than it should have been. A rasp against that pulse of need between them, that intense current. "It's statistically impossible."

"The only failures I've ever had all share one thing in

common," she said, and the heat between them pulled taut.
Grew hotter. Wilder. Pounded in him. He saw it move in
her gaze, across her face. "Guess what that is?"

"They didn't do what you told them to do. To continue
the theme."

"Look at that." There was that flash in her gray gaze that
he felt like the touch he craved, like a burst of fire deep in
his gut. Did he move closer? Did she? He couldn't tell any
longer. "He can be taught."

Hunter could see the awareness and arousal on her face
then, like a flashing sign. That faint hint of color high on
her cheeks, that sheen in her eyes. That sudden, almost
shocking hint of softness in her lips. It took every bit of
willpower he had to keep from bending down and tasting
it. Tasting her.

Drinking her in and getting good and drunk on her heat.
Making her feel that clench of fire that was driving him
mad. Filling the hollow places inside him with the flames.

Letting them both burn.

He liked the way her chin tilted up, tough and cool despite the clamor and slap of the flames that danced in the
air all around them. He liked the fierce kick of his own
desire, all of that feeling when he'd been so numb for so
long. He wanted to test it against hers, see what it made of
them. See if they survived. How long they'd burn before
they broke. He *wanted*.

"Do you want to play teacher?" he asked, drawing the
words out, because he liked the way his voice worked in

her, half tease, half promise. He could see it in the way she fought to hide it. He could feel it inside, hard and hot. "Because I have some ideas for the first lesson. I think you'll like the exercises. But first you have to tell me why I'm here."

For a moment, Zoe couldn't remember.

What they were talking about, what was happening, what she was—or wasn't—doing. Hunter was like a wall before her, imposing and huge, and shockingly, irrepressibly male.

And hot. So hot it almost hurt to be this close to him, burning alive when she'd worked so hard to stay icy through and through. So hot she was afraid she'd lose herself forever if she didn't do something—anything—to keep from falling into the wildfire that seemed to rage in the tiny little space between their bodies.

Think, she ordered herself the way she'd learned to do in far worse situations than this one. *Don't simply* react. *Think this through.*

But that was very hard to do when she was surrounded by a big, hard, beautiful man—who was looking at her as if he'd like to eat her whole. As if he already knew how she tasted. As if all she needed to do was give the slightest little bit of an inch, and she could find out herself.

Not that she wanted something like that. Like him. Of course she didn't.

But right now, right here, it was difficult to remember why not.

"Mr. Grant," she said, her voice a cold blast of winter,

folding her arms over her chest in a way that was obviously a defensive gesture—but it couldn't be helped. She was only human. Even if Hunter Grant was, improbably, the first client who had ever made her feel like this. The first *man* who'd come close, in too many years to count. Maybe ever, and she didn't want to think about the implications of that. "I think you have the wrong idea."

"Don't lie to me, Zoe." She didn't know what was worse—the laughter in his voice, the blaze of intense heat in his gaze, or the unexpected caress of her name in his mouth. That smug, male, somehow intoxicating mouth that she absolutely was not imagining claiming hers. "Persuade. Pivot, if you must. But don't stoop to *lying*."

He was daring her.

"Mr. Grant," she said again, on a theatrically exasperated sigh, as if he was a naughty schoolboy, "you could try the patience of one of your saints."

"Lucky, then, that none are in this room."

"I don't have to resort to lies." She relaxed against the desk, as if she'd never been more at her ease. As if she routinely had very large men entirely too close to her, moments away from a kiss she suspected she'd do better to avoid—that might, she worried, shake her whole world apart, and then what would happen to her great plans for Jason Treffen? "It may surprise you to discover that you're not the first of my clients to imagine that injecting sex into the situation might make this process more palatable for them."

One of those dark, unreadable expressions of his moved

across his face, suggesting—again—that he was an enor-
mously complicated man. Far more complicated than he
liked to let on, and she still didn't want to believe that was
possible. Because it would make everything she needed to
do with him much more difficult. He smiled, sending that
dancing, seductive fire to wild heights inside her. Making
her belly hollow out, then pull taut.

"Is that what I'm doing?" he asked, in a light tone she
didn't believe for a moment. "But then, maybe those clients actually hired you."

Hunter shifted back on his heels, then shoved his thumbs
into the pockets of yet another pair of jeans that fit him
much too well. The movement made his finely cut button-
down shirt pull taut against the smooth, solid muscles of
his chest, and thanks to her bright idea to confront him in
that hot tub, she knew exactly what was behind the fabric. Zoe found her throat felt tight. And worse, she felt that
extra sliver of space yawn between them as if it was a loss.
As if it was grief.

"You don't have to hire me, Mr. Grant. I've generously
decided to take your case on pro bono."

"Be still my heart."

Hers was making a racket. "But we were talking about
sex."

"Were we? How exciting. I thought we were discussing
image rehab." But his bright eyes were too hot and much
too assessing on hers.

"No, you didn't." She wished his smile didn't lance into

her like that. That she wasn't so shockingly susceptible to a man like this, when she would have believed that impossible only a week ago. "Here's the thing. You're obviously an attractive man."

"Thank you." His tone was dry, but she didn't change the steady way she was watching him, as if she was delivering a lecture from a podium. If she did it long enough, maybe she'd tamp down that riot inside her, too. "All those magazine covers can't be wrong, I flatter myself."

He ran a hand down his front, making it difficult to hear herself think over the sudden noise in her brain, her body. Her skin. Her bones. There was only the slow journey of his palm over the ridged, solid wonder of his abdomen, as if he was smoothing out a wrinkle from his shirt, which, she was well aware, he was not.

She'd seen him wet and almost naked the other night, rising from that hot tub like a fever dream. The lean muscles, the ridged abdomen, the arrow of dark, male hair that pointed south. It was pressed into her memory like a red-hot brand.

It was suddenly hard to swallow, but she forced herself to do it. Then to push on as if his little display hadn't unsettled her at all.

"Your former job demanded a level of physical fitness that's impressive, and I'd be lying if I said it wasn't intriguing, on some level."

"And you don't lie. Thank goodness."

"But you're a very specific sort of man." She smiled when

he frowned at that. "Most of the men who walk into this office are more or less the same. You're used to being in control, you told me so yourself. You may or may not find me attractive, but you'd have sex with me anyway because in your mind, doing so would put me back in the subordinate position you think I ought to be in. You're the kind of man who gets off on that. And as a bonus, you'd get to keep feeling in control no matter how many times I told you to do things for the cameras that you didn't like."

"Well," he said, and there was a considering sort of gleam in the deep blue of his gaze then, and a great tide of that insane heat that she was pretending she didn't notice, "and it would also be fun."

She'd been hoping he'd say something like that.

"Not for me," she told him, her eyes on his. Direct and matter-of-fact. And, she knew, about to end this thing once and for all.

Because Zoe had never had a client come on to her yet who didn't back off when she threw some version of this speech at them. She told herself that strange stabbing feeling in the vicinity of her chest was too much coffee, not the faint disappointment that Hunter was just one more among the multitudes. Interchangeable assholes, all of them, like the fleets of yellow cabs racing down Ninth Avenue outside her windows, wholly indistinguishable from one another.

Which was why she'd chosen him, she reminded herself. Because he was just like the rest. Just like the worst.

"I'm afraid I wasn't kidding when I told you that I prefer

to be the one in charge." She watched his face as her words penetrated. "You might be pretty, but I don't want you—or anyone—unless you crawl. And that isn't a metaphor."

Everything went still.

Excruciatingly still.

Hunter's intelligent blue gaze was much too hot, and Zoe felt an odd constriction grip her, as if something hard and tight was wrapped around her ribs, the way some insane and rebellious part of her wished his hands were.

Moments ticked by, and Hunter didn't do any of the usual, expected things. He didn't scoff. He didn't argue. He didn't bluster or recoil or toss insults at her head.

He simply...watched her. Studied her. Making her realize, with his intent silence, that she underestimated this man at her peril. It was unnerving. She was beginning to think _he_ was unnerving, and she didn't understand how he'd managed to convince the world that he was nothing but a jock—

And then he smiled, shattering the moment and making her heart flip inside her chest.

"Okay," he said.

She was so shaken she almost stammered out her reply, and she never would have forgiven herself if she had. She sucked in a breath, fighting for control. What the hell was happening to her? What was next—tears? A child's screaming fit on the floor? She could suddenly see the appeal of both.

"I don't understand what that means," she said, when she could speak calmly.

"It means…okay."

What was that dark, hungry thing in his gaze that she could feel burrowing into her, making her edgy and something like nervous, with that clenching feeling low in her belly? *What was this?* By this point, any other man she'd ever had pursue her like this would have veered off into a temper tantrum—proving once and for all that what they wanted was her surrender, however they could get it.

Not her. Never *her*. Just the power rush of having her submit to them, one way or another.

She didn't understand Hunter at all. It made her nervous, down deep into parts of her she'd assumed nothing could ever touch, all those dark and hidden pockets she'd thought she'd walled off and locked away for good.

"'Okay?'" she echoed. "Are you really telling me that you, Hunter Talbot Grant III, the John McEnroe of football and the most loathed celebrity of our time, secretly harbor submissive fantasies? You—the very poster boy for chest-beating, alpha-male assholes?"

He grinned, wolfish again, every inch of him a dangerous predator, too hot and too hungry, and if she hadn't had both her feet firmly on the floor, Zoe would have sworn her whole office was spinning all around her in jagged, drunken loops.

"Sure," he said, with that cocky twist to his lips and a conquering gleam in his bright blue gaze. "I don't like labels, Ms. Brook. I like to win. Does that make me submissive?"

She'd never seen a less submissive creature in her entire life.

There was no way this man—who oozed Neanderthal from his very pores, who had made a spectacle of himself and his inability to be told what to do, ever, by anyone, even when it was *his job* to do what his coaches told him—was capable of even the *pretense* of surrender.

He thought this was a game. He thought *everything* was a game. But that didn't mean he'd win.

"Fine, then." She felt the clamor in her chest, the pulse of all that heat below, but focused instead on calling his bluff, because that was all that mattered. "Then what are you waiting for? The office door is closed. Your secret's safe with me. By all means, be beta."

He only watched her, still and focused, wildly male and intensely demanding without saying a word. He didn't have to speak. He emanated command and iron control from every single one of those perfectly hewn, mouthwateringly smooth muscles. From his beautiful eyes, his tough jaw. Even the way he stood there before her, formidably appealing and still too close, whispered to that tender, feminine place inside her she thought Jason Treffen had killed off years ago.

Hunter made her feel *soft,* and that was unforgivable.

So she snapped her fingers and pointed at the floor.

"Be a good boy, Hunter. Crawl."

And the way he laughed then was like a lit match to a flood of gasoline, catapulting them both into a raging inferno Zoe worried—with a desperate surge of panic—would consume them both right then and there. It rolled through her, touching every part of her with flame and wonder and a kind of fear. It made her shiver. It made her want to call this off before it got any worse—

But she didn't move. She didn't speak. *She couldn't back down.* She couldn't let him see her consider it.

Hunter inclined his head slightly, almost regally, holding her gaze with his.

Knowing. Demanding.

Pure male challenge cloaked in all that searing blue.

"Ask and you shall receive," he said in a voice that went straight to her head, and between her legs, and was about as far from submissive as it was possible to be.

Because *he* was about as submissive as an actual alpha wolf.

And then he opened his arms wide in a parody of surrender wholly belied by that mocking curve to his perfect lips, took a step back and then dropped to his knees—right there in the middle of her office.

Chapter Four

Zoe's breath deserted her in a rush, then came too hard, too fast.

Her body felt like someone else's, as if her heart beat that wild and rough of its own volition, as if it wanted to tear its way out of her chest all on its own. It was an insistent pulse in her throat, her belly. In her suddenly too-heavy breasts and that shocking, swollen heat between her legs.

She felt as if he'd punched her. Some part of her wished he had. She was only dimly aware that she'd dropped her hands to her sides and was gripping the edge of her glass-topped desk.

Hard, as if she was afraid of what might happen if she let go.

As if she already knew exactly what would happen.

Because the only thing she could see was Hunter. The crisp bright winter daylight faded away, New York ceased to exist outside her windows, the business she'd made and the revenge she was determined to enact disappeared like smoke.

There was nothing but Hunter.

On his knees in front of her, big and male and that lazy, frankly sensual look in his beautiful eyes that his technically submissive position did nothing at all to undercut. He was such a large man that even kneeling, his head was nearly at the level of her breasts, and her nipples went painfully hard at the notion of what he could do with that.

What she *wanted* him to do—but no. She couldn't want that, could she? She wasn't the kind of woman who *wanted*. She wasn't sure she knew how. That was only one among the many things she'd lost. That had been taken from her.

The very thought of her sordid, ugly past should have spurred her into some kind of action, a better defense at the very least, but she couldn't seem to make herself move.

Hunter looked as if he was *this close* to simply leaning in and tasting her, taking her—simply because he could, simply because he was *Hunter*—no matter that she was theoretically standing in the power position. Literally looking down at him.

It should have made a difference. It should have wrecked a man like him right down to the marrow of his alpha male bones.

Clearly, it wasn't working.

If anything, Zoe felt even more like his prey than she had when he was looming over her, taking up all of her space, making her frighteningly unable to tell the difference between his breath and hers…

Oh, yes. She was in trouble.

And she still couldn't control her breathing.

"Your wish is my command, Zoe," he said, that rich current of amusement in his low voice, his eyes never shifting from hers. Her traitorous hands itched to close the distance between them, to bury themselves in the thickness of his dark blond hair, and that trickle of yearning that was very nearly an urge came much too close to overwhelming her. She didn't understand it. She certainly didn't want it. "Please tell me those shoes you're wearing are involved in whatever dominatrix fantasies you'd like to play out. I promise, I'm happy to be your willing slave."

"This is ridiculous." Her voice was a hiss of sound. Desperate, she could hear, and could only hope he didn't know *how* desperate. "You're playing games."

"Be on top, if you want," he said in that sinful drawl of his that shivered through her, making it hard to sit still on the edge of her desk. Or at all. His gaze burned into hers. "I don't care. Whatever turns you on."

She didn't want to think about what turned her on. It had never really come up before—not like this. It was as if Hunter knew more about her body, her desires and her needs, than she did. As if he was deliberately provoking her, as if he knew precisely how little it would take to tip her over into a great blaze.

"I need you to stop this," she said sternly—or as sternly as she could. "That's what turns me on. You on your feet, an appropriate distance away from me, behaving yourself."

But he moved then. He tilted his glorious body forward,

and caged her hips in his big, sure hands, and everything seemed to explode. Or that was only her—a great, white-hot, rolling sort of implosion, tearing her apart from the inside out. There was so much *heat*—

From his strong, elegant hands. From that hard, male look on his face. From *her*—inside her. All the pieces of her she was sure would fly apart into a thousand shattered bits if he hadn't been holding her fast between his hands, making her flush from head to toe, red and wild and terrified.

And then Hunter simply reached down, took the hem of her skirt in his remarkably agile, hard and calloused hands, and began to ease it up her legs.

"You can't— What are you—"

She was stammering, and the worst part was, she didn't care the way she had a few moments ago. Now it was the least of her worries.

"Worshipping you." Hunter's voice was a low growl that made her skin tingle, the hair at the back of her neck stand on end, and gooseflesh prickle into life in all the places she'd gone red. "All good surrenders begin with an act of worship, Zoe. Everyone knows that."

And for a moment, she only stared down at him, stunned. Frozen. Doing *absolutely nothing* while this man pushed her skirt higher and higher, holding her gaze all the while.

For a sizzling moment, they only stared at each other.

Then Hunter slid one hand around the back of her right thigh, holding it still while the rest of her shuddered. He held her gaze for another endless moment—and then he bent, put his lips to her flesh, and sucked. Hard.

It hurt. It was like a spike of fire, punching into her, from that spot high on her thigh to the melting heat above, then outward to every lost and yearning part of her, making her entire body *his,* not hers. It was like nothing she'd ever felt before.

It was, she realized from some great distance where her brain worked despite the clamor and riot of all of this, a fucking *hickey.* He pulled back, his hands still in dangerous places on her thighs, his mouth in a smug crook, and that sting stamped into her skin.

He'd *marked* her.

And now he looked up at her again, unrepentant and determined, his hands moving up again, deliberate and slow. His next goal obvious.

So obvious, she thought she might drown in her own fire.

So deliciously, heatedly obvious, she knew that if she let this go on for a single second more, he would own her. She would be lost forever, and he would know that with a simple act like this one, he could have whatever he wanted from her.

That was what did it.

Zoe pushed away from the desk, too aware that he *let* her bat his hands away from her skirt, from those whisper-like touches to the tender skin above her knees that she told herself meant nothing, *did* nothing. She stepped away from him in an undignified hurry that almost made her trip over her own feet, moving behind the desk in what she hoped looked like temper.

Because she didn't know what she'd do if he saw the depth of her panic. If he knew how close he'd come to destroying her, and worse, how close she'd been to letting him.

She wasn't sure he hadn't.

"You can stay on your knees, Mr. Grant," she bit out, as if calling him that could erase what he'd done, or allow her to believe in her own strength again the way she wanted—*needed*—to do. "It suits you. Maybe you'll learn a little humility down there."

"It's unlikely."

He rose with that innate, athletic grace that reminded her what feats of strength he was capable of performing, if he chose. He was like some kind of warrior, easy and something like beautiful despite the solid, heavy width of his shoulders, the smooth power he wore so easily, the capacity for all of that brutality in every hard line.

When had she stopped finding him disgusting?

"If you touch me again," she told him, holding his gaze so there was no mistake, no possible misinterpretation, and hoped her gaze was clearer than her head, "I will not only launch a campaign to ruin you even further, I'll be tempted to report you to the proper authorities."

He laughed, and it swept through her like a new kind of fire, swallowing everything in its path.

"Nothing like a complete overreaction to prove that you're not quite as cold as you'd like me to think, Zoe."

"You manhandled me. This is an underreaction."

"Then you should have told me to stop." His gaze hurt, it was so hot. "You didn't."

And for the first time in as long as she could remember, Zoe couldn't find the proper retort to slap him back into place. She simply stood there, the city behind her and the life she'd built all around her like so much set dressing, staring at the man who was supposed to be a tool she used, not... *this.* Not a certain path to her own destruction.

She could *see* it. She felt the mark he'd left on her body, like a sweet hot burn.

Like shame.

"If you won't tell me why you want me, I'll have to assume this is a particularly creative campaign to get into my bed," he said, folding his arms over his broad chest and looking entirely too male and arrogant and self-satisfied. *Smug,* she thought. "And I like sex, Zoe. A lot. So I'm happy to crawl around on the floor if that's what it takes. What do I care? But if I do, you're going to have to admit that you want me just as much. That this is all a complicated ploy to get naked with me."

"I don't." It was automatic. And much too fast. "And this isn't a ploy."

He considered her. "Or I can just do what I usually do. You'll huff and puff and call me all kinds of names. Neanderthal, cretin, asshole, whatever."

"I believe the word you're looking for is *misogynistic.*"

"That, too. Not that it's true. Not that you think it's true, either, but far be it from me to get in the way of your wishful thinking. We'll end up in the same place either way."

His gaze dropped then, tracing over her cheeks, her mouth. Moving lower, and spreading that terrible heat wherever it touched, as potent as if he'd used his hands. The places his fingers had brushed her skin, all along her inner thighs, burned red hot. And made her glad the wide expanse of her desk was between them now.

She realized then that she didn't know if she'd push him away if he came close again, and that was the most terrifying realization she'd had so far.

"This isn't 'huffing and puffing,' Mr. Grant," Zoe told him as icily as she could. "The truth is, I don't find these displays of yours at all attractive."

Hunter stared at her for a long, dark, infinitely tense and dangerous moment, until there was no pretending her cheeks hadn't flushed even redder than before, or that he couldn't see that flagrant evidence right there before him, like a flag.

Showing him what a liar she was.

She was only happy he couldn't feel that bite of his the way she could, throbbing and kicking at her, telling her a thousand things she didn't want to know, and all of them a story of her own appalling weakness.

"Yes, Zoe," he said then, in a mocking little murmur that echoed inside her like a terrible shiver, the ruin of her right there in the gleam of those too-blue eyes, the perilous curve of his mouth. "I think you do."

* * *

"So you hate him," her coworker Daniel said later that afternoon, scowling across the office's snug kitchenette in the wake of Zoe's ill-advised and bad-tempered little rant on the topic of Hunter and his many image problems. To say nothing of his personal problems. To say nothing of *her* problems—though she hadn't mentioned that part. Much less the mark he'd left on her, like evidence. "I hate him, too. The entire world hates him. I believe his own team burned him in effigy at the Super Bowl halftime show. So why, may I ask, are you taking him on as a client?"

You, Zoe noted. Not the *we* he usually used. Daniel was making a point.

"I don't like him," Zoe said carefully, trying—too late—to modify her tone and hide her panic, "but it's not personal. I just don't like football." She let out a small laugh and decided she really didn't need coffee after all. "That's not even true, technically—I don't know anything about football." Except that her grandfather had treated it like his religion, had made the entire house his place of worship—and woe betide anyone who diverted his attention from his television screen, at any point during the endless football season. "I've managed to make my entire adult life a sports-free zone, in fact."

"Do we need this kind of challenge?" Daniel asked, tightly. His gaze was filled with accusation and temper. "Did you come up with a new mission statement? Take the most reprehensible human beings around and see if you can make them soft and cuddly and suitable for public consumption?"

"He has a temper and some impulse-control issues," Zoe replied, furious that Daniel was goading her into *defending* Hunter Grant. Even more furious that she was actually doing it. "He got fired from his job because of some anger-management issues. That makes him *slightly* less reprehensible than, say, child molesters? Terrorists? Don't you think?"

Daniel only stared at her, a mulish set to his jaw, a light she didn't want to acknowledge in his gaze.

"Problem?" she asked. As mildly as she could.

"I don't like the way he looks at you," Daniel said. Too fast, as if he'd been wanting to say it since he'd dropped in to discuss a few campaign logistics with the two of them in Zoe's office earlier. While Zoe had sat there pretending to be professional with a freaking hickey on her thigh and Hunter had done nothing but smirk. "And I really don't like the fact you don't seem to *mind* the way he looks at you."

This was her fault. She'd walked right into this, and Zoe bit back a sigh as he glared at her, slipping her right hand up to her opposite shoulder and squeezing hard against the tension there that made her neck feel as unyielding as rebar. Daniel had been her first hire when she'd started her own company four years ago, an easy choice to make after knowing him since her earliest days in PR.

But Daniel was more than that. He was the first man she'd let herself trust—on any level—after escaping from Jason Treffen.

And one night in Park City, Utah, while managing a hotshot director's post-cocaine addiction revival at the Sundance Film Festival, she'd let the fact she liked him and trusted him slip over a line she should have held fast.

That had been a year ago, and she'd paid for that mistake in a variety of ways ever since. Apparently, this afternoon would be another form of payment.

"I need you to be my associate, Daniel," she said softly now, holding his gaze even though she didn't particularly want to hold it. But she thought she owed him that much. "My coworker. Not a jealous boyfriend."

"I'm not your boyfriend." There was no disguising the bitterness then. It made his mouth look fierce and fragile all at once, and his whole lean, rangy body tensed. "It was one kiss. You ended it, not me—"

"And this is exactly why," she bit out, an icy thrust of the knife, her aim true.

Daniel's green eyes flared with temper, and something else she didn't want to face, but then he looked away. He blew out a breath. Zoe dug her fingers harder into the side of her neck—half massage, half punishment—and let the fact she was *such a liar* swirl around her like a cape. Like shame, again.

Like that telltale burn, that mark on her thigh.

It wasn't some sense of her responsibility as Daniel's boss that had made her push him away that night at Sundance. It wasn't any fear over what their working relationship might have become if she'd let that kiss go where he'd wanted it to go. She wished it had been. She'd let Daniel think it had been, because either of those things would have been better than the truth.

Which was this: she'd felt nothing.

She'd thought what had happened to her, what she'd done because she'd had to do it, had left her frigid. Unable to feel anything at all, even when an objectively good-looking man she *liked,* who she considered one of her few friends in this world, wanted her. When she'd thought she wanted that, wanted him, too.

Daniel adored her; she'd known that for years. He was good, kind. Perfect for her—and she'd felt *nothing.* She'd thought that was yet another part of the price she'd already spent so long paying, for the cardinal sin of being a naive idiot at the age of twenty-two.

She'd thought she was broken on a fundamental level. Beyond repair or salvation. Ruined straight through.

Until today.

Not everything is a joke, she'd thrown at Hunter back in her office, after he'd left her standing there, stunned, and had walked over to the couch and thrown himself down on it as if nothing had happened. When she'd been wrecked. In pieces.

He'd studied her for a moment, that gorgeous face of his somber. Not joking at all.

Tell me what you want from me, he'd said quietly. *Or tell me what you're afraid of. Your choice.*

And Zoe still didn't know how to handle that. The fact

that Hunter Grant was the only person she'd met in years who saw the truth. Who saw what she hid beneath her tough-as-nails exterior. Hunter Grant, who could have pressed his advantage today, but hadn't.

She didn't understand that, either. And it certainly wasn't something she could discuss with Daniel, who might love her, she knew, but had never *seen* her. Not the way Hunter had. Not all of her.

Zoe knew the storm had passed between them when Daniel let out a short laugh.

"Fine," he muttered. "I get it."

He looked at her then, that male awareness she didn't want to see edged out by concern. Unlike Hunter in every possible way. Daniel might not *see* her, but he cared for her. Why couldn't that be enough?

But she knew.

In a way, it even made sense. She was tarnished straight through, stained by the things she'd done, and she knew it. She'd accepted it a long time ago. It stood to reason, in an awful sort of way, that the only man who could make her feel anything had been crafted directly from a selection of her darkest fears. He was the kind of man she hated the most. The kind of man who would revel in that sort of power over her, she had no doubt. He'd already started.

That mark on her thigh seemed to glow, then ache.

"I don't like this, Zoe," Daniel said now, reminding her where she was, and with whom. "I think he's dangerous."

"Of course he's dangerous," she said lightly, and even

laughed. Pretended it didn't hurt. That none of it hurt. "That's why it's our job to make him into a cuddly little kitten."

Step one of which started tomorrow, and called for a lot more alone time with the man. The very last thing Zoe wanted.

But she would do it, she knew. Because she had no choice. Because her revenge was more important than anything else, including her own feelings, and she would make it work.

She didn't have a choice.

Hunter drove into the depressing town some two hours from Manhattan that Zoe directed him to, mystified and annoyed. All around them were crumbling brick buildings, the oppressive air of deeply saturated despair, all the usual ruins of what had once been a mill town. Similar places dotted the East Coast, he knew, none of them particularly appealing all these years after the last gasp of the textile industry. This was the most time he'd spent in one, and he already wanted to leave.

"This looks like a lovely place to live," he said, staring out the window at the small, desolate-looking row houses that lined the street, looking abandoned in the weak light of the winter afternoon, though he suspected they weren't. "So welcoming."

"Let's stop at a Realtor's on the way out," Zoe retorted, and she let out a small noise that was too sharp to be a laugh. "You can buy a house or two with your pocket change."

"What are we doing?" he asked, not as softly as he had the first time, right after he'd picked her up outside her office this afternoon. Or even the fifth time, when they'd picked up I-95 at the George Washington Bridge and headed north. "Why are we here?"

"You're going to have to wait and see," she said, her cool tone perfectly even, as it had been this whole time. Her attention was on her BlackBerry, her thumbs tapping at the keys. "You might even have to trust me." She glanced at him and her lips curved slightly. Almost sharply. "Turn right at the light."

Hunter didn't trust her. He didn't even trust himself. But he'd tasted her. He'd felt the sweet smooth heat of her skin beneath his hands. He'd smelled her heady scent, lavender and woman, hot and needy. He wanted more.

He wanted answers, too. But he wanted her more.

He turned right at the light, and followed her directions all the way to the parking lot of an old, unrenovated high school building on the far side of town. Edgarton High read the weathered sign on the nearest wall. He parked with what he could admit was a slightly showy screech of his tires, though it elicited zero reaction from Zoe. He beckoned her out of his car, but, naturally, she didn't do as directed. She turned to look at him instead, to study him as if he was a painting on the wall of some second-rate art gallery and she didn't quite see the point. He felt the punch of her gaze again, the electricity, and it pissed him off.

If this was about sex, the way he wanted it to be, they

would have had sex by now. A lot of it. And he didn't want to think about what else it could be about, because she didn't seem inclined to answer and he wasn't entirely sure he wanted to know.

She sat there, elegant and aloof, her long legs crossed and her hands folded neatly in her lap. Only her eyes seemed warm—hot, really, and far too calculating as they moved over him. Judging him and dismissing him and making sure he was aware of it while she did it.

"Are you familiar with the concept of a hate fuck?" he asked.

She smirked. Of course she smirked, though he flattered himself that maybe, just maybe, there was the slightest flush over her lovely cheeks as she did. What did it say about him that he wanted to believe that? With an urgency that felt a little too close to desperation?

"How awkward," Zoe said, though she didn't sound anything like awkward. "I don't hate you, Mr. Grant. This is called *indifference*."

"Don't worry," he told her shortly, not bothering to hide his bad temper, if that was what it was. It felt like ground glass in his throat, his gut. And even lower, as if he was still a fifteen-year-old idiot. "I can hate you enough for the both of us."

"You don't hate me." She was remarkably, unflappably confident, which he really shouldn't find arousing. And yet. "You can't understand why I'm not fluttering about in awe and wonder at the great gift of your attention, and the only way a man like you can interpret that is with your..." She eyed the area in question, which didn't help improve matters, then raised her gaze to his. Hers was like the winter sea, and much too amused besides. "Well. I'll just say no, thank you, and leave it at that."

"Just as well," he muttered. "I have the feeling you'd be a messy crier. And yes, they usually cry. Tears of joy and wonder. It's my gift."

"I wouldn't brag that you kiss the girls and make them cry, Mr. Grant," she replied at once, the only person he'd ever met who was so cheerfully immune to him. He told himself the way that made him feel—that jostling inside him, scraping at him from the inside out—was happy. Perfectly fucking happy. "There are words for men like that, and some of those words come with jail time."

"Are we going to sit here all day?" he growled.

She only laughed and started to open her door, leaving Hunter to jerk his attention away from her smart-ass mouth and heave himself out of the low-slung car before he did yet another thing he'd regret.

Zoe exited with far more grace, seeming wholly unperturbed by the fact her jet black boots sported high, wicked heels and the parking lot beneath them was more ice than asphalt. And then she *sauntered* toward him. There was no other word for it. She was a menace, he was hard, and he was deeply and utterly disgusted with this whole situation. With himself.

Was this really an improvement over *numb?*

"Why do you great big men insist on driving these tiny little cars?" she asked. He was coming apart at the seams while this infuriating woman was *chatting* as if she was at a boring cocktail party and she'd decided to grit her teeth and be polite to him. "You practically have to lie down to get in it. Surely with all the money you have at your disposal you could find a sports car that you actually *fit* in."

"I like fast cars," he said. "And the faster they are, the smaller they are. It's simple aerodynamics."

In a minute he'd be beating his chest like an ape. Or doing exactly what he wanted to do, what he'd effectively warned her he might do, which was drag her off to the nearest cave with his hands sunk deep into that glossy swing of her dark hair.

And then. *And then.*

But she was laughing at him. Arch. Aloof. And still he wanted her.

"Just follow me, please," she said with all of that infuriating calm. "And try not to trip over anything while you're busy looking down your nose at how the simple folk live."

"Can you really just...*walk in?*" he asked when she threw open the heavy door to the school and ushered him through it with an incline of her pretty head. "Shouldn't there be guards or something?"

"This isn't the kind of place where the community rallies around and demands security measures at the high school," she said, her tone slightly more icy than before. "It's more the kind of place where meth use is on the rise, everyone drinks their considerable troubles away in the depressing local bars, and the only thing you can possibly do to survive is get out. But then, very few people manage to do that."

"Thank you so much for bringing me here," he said, not even trying to contain his irritation. "Nothing I enjoy more than—"

"This is where Sarah came from," Zoe said, her voice like a knife through the quiet hallway. Hunter thought he turned to stone, or maybe he only wished he had. Zoe's cool gaze searched his, and there was a kind of dark heat there he didn't recognize—but she blinked it away. Then treated him to that edgy, demanding smile. "This is the high school she went to. She was valedictorian that year. That's how she got into Harvard. Did you know that?"

He knew parts of it. But there was a terrible foreboding gripping him then, like a hard hand on his throat, and he didn't want to have this conversation. He didn't want any part of this. He didn't want to know more than he already did.

"No," he said. "I didn't." Because that was close enough to the truth.

"How long were you two together?"

"You could at least *try* to keep the judgment out of your tone."

She laughed, a hollow sound. "That was me trying."

"Try harder," he suggested. He eyed her for a minute. "Or find a different ghost to keep throwing in my face." He didn't understand the multitude of shadows he saw cross her face then. He didn't want to understand, much as he didn't want to ask the next question. But he did. "Are you going to tell me how you knew her?"

Zoe didn't answer, and the coward in him was relieved. She started walking and he wanted to leave, there and then. He wanted nothing to do with this sharp, edgy woman who hid her softness so deep, much less those dark things he'd seen in her storm-tossed eyes. Nothing about her—nothing about *this*—would lead him back to numbness, and that was the only thing he knew how to do. The only thing he wanted.

Yet Hunter followed her anyway.

The school was a mess. Dingy walls, peeling paint. No facilities to speak of, or none that hadn't seen their glory days a long, long time ago. It was a far cry from the exclusive prep school he'd attended outside Boston. This was a place where dreams were pounded down into dust, then denied. The apathy soaked into the walls, echoed down the dim corridors, burrowed under Hunter's skin and made him feel guilty with every step. Guilti-*er.*

Sarah had walked here. She'd lived through this, and somehow, when he'd met her at Harvard, she'd been like a live wire. Not beaten down. Not crushed. She'd *bristled* with all the dreams she'd planned to make real, and she'd insisted that everyone around her do the same.

If it hadn't been for Sarah, he'd have taken the path of least resistance straight into the hedge fund his father ran in Boston, a path his younger brother had followed without a murmur. He'd have lived the life Zoe Brook had laid out for him in that strip club, all Monopoly money and *Mayflower* blue bloods like his sister, Nora, and her snooty art charity their parents were happy to subsidize, because that was what he'd always been expected to do. He was a Grant, and Grants were financiers. Businessmen. Occasional philanthropists, not professional athletes. Such vulgar displays were beneath them, as his mother had only stopped reminding him after his third or fourth much-publicized scandal.

It had been Sarah who'd told him he should do what he wanted to do, not what his family expected him to do. And who knew what his life might have been like if he'd handled things differently ten years ago? Maybe he would have saved Sarah from her nightmare. Maybe then he would have taken pride in the dream she'd encouraged him to make real and done something other than waste it.

But he'd never know now.

He stopped walking when Zoe did, and saw they stood outside an empty gymnasium and the sad little weight room with broken blinds that abutted it. He frowned through the glass, and it took a moment for him to understand that he wasn't angry, despite the kick of something a lot like anger in his blood. If anything, he was defensive.

He was so tense it actually hurt.

"That's the high school football team," Zoe told him. "Such as it is."

He stared at the kids on the other side of the window. They didn't look anything like a football team. They were scrawny. There wasn't a natural athlete in the group, something that was painfully evident even at a cursory glance.

That foreboding feeling was starting to choke him again, and harder this time.

Hunter raked his hands through his hair, agitated. He wanted to move. *Do* something. This restlessness was his undoing. It always had been. It led him to fight or fuck, no matter what his brain told him to do. He doubted Zoe would appreciate either.

She was very still beside him. Too still. It tripped all kinds of alarms in him, but he didn't understand why, and he liked that about as much as that restless thing inside him, still kicking at him.

She pointed at the young teacher in the corner, talking intensely to one of the students.

"That's Jack," she said. "He teaches math and I'm pretty sure the only thing he knows about football he watched on YouTube. He bought most of the weights in there himself and pretended he'd found the money for it somewhere in the athletic programs budget, which, let's be clear, doesn't exist in a place like this."

"Is this a charity thing?" he asked after a moment. "Because I didn't have to drive two hours into the hinterland to hear another fucking sob story. I could have written you a check in your office yesterday."

"This isn't a charity."

"Then what? Why am I here?"

She frowned at him when he turned to look at her, and

there was a storm he didn't understand in her gaze, turning it a dark, rich gray. Making him wish—but that was ridiculous. Insane. If he reached out to her she'd probably amputate his hand with a single glare.

"For all you know, one of these kids is the next—" She stopped. "I have no idea what constitutes a football prodigy. You? Maybe one of them is the next you."

Hunter wouldn't wish that on anyone, much less a kid who already had nothing.

"There are no prodigies in that room," he said flatly. "This football team sucks. And yes, that's an assessment I feel comfortable making without having seen even one of them throw a ball."

Her eyes were too dark to bear.

"Lucky, then, that they have one of the best players in football history at their disposal. You can teach them how to throw a ball."

"No." He sounded far away, even to himself. "I can't."

"You will."

He let out a sound that was far too stark to be a laugh.

"I watched *Friday Night Lights,* too," he said. "Everybody loves Coach Taylor, Zoe. But that doesn't mean I want to become him."

"No one's in any danger of confusing you with Coach Taylor," she retorted, and though that darkness was still in her gaze, her voice sounded the way it always did. Smooth. Cool. A challenge he felt like her hands against his skin, his dick. "Coach Taylor is a beloved figure no one wants to believe is fictional. Not to mention, a good man."

"My point exactly," he gritted out. "The last thing these kids need is me."

He thought she pulled in a breath then, sharp and quick, and it hinted that maybe she wasn't as cool as she appeared.

It was pathetic how much he wanted that to be true.

"This is called damage control," she told him. "The real-life equivalent of a bad guy in a movie cuddling a fluffy little puppy. We need to humanize you. You're too rich and too hated."

"The paparazzi will find me." He didn't know why he was so angry, why he felt so raw. So attacked. So unequal to this, in every way. "They always do. I can already see the headlines. My cynical attempt to turn the tide of public favor. My calculated maneuver to win back my fans. And so on. There's no way I'll look like anything but a posturing asshole."

"Let me worry about that."

"I don't want this," he snapped at her. "I'm bored enough to let my dick lead me halfway up the Eastern Seaboard, but I'm not going to pretend to be some kind of positive influence on a pack of kids. The hypocrisy might actually kill me. You're going to have to find someone else to play your little games, Zoe."

"No." Was that alarm he saw on her face? Did he merely want it to be? "I need you."

"Too bad."

"This is the first step," she said quickly, and he had the sense that she wanted to reach out and put a hand on his arm—but didn't. Because they both knew what happened when they touched.

And he was enough of an animal that he let that soothe him, that hint that she was as thrown by the fire between them as he was.

She was quiet for a long time, though he could feel her there beside him, that edginess of hers seeming to vibrate, to make the air shake around them. To sneak its way into him, too, as if she was burrowing beneath his skin, when that was the last thing he wanted.

Hunter had to fight to keep himself from reaching over and looping an arm around her slender body, pulling her close to him, as if she needed or wanted his warmth. He didn't even know where that urge came from. He'd been tender with exactly one person in his entire life, and he was still dealing with the wreckage. He wouldn't make that mistake again.

"Do this," she said finally, her voice low, when he'd started to think she wouldn't speak at all. "Do it and watch what I can do when I leak it, how quickly opinion about you changes. I'm that good."

"And this is your big plan? You're wasting your time. Because I don't care what they say about me, Zoe. I'm immune."

"I don't believe you," she said, so soft it was almost a whisper.

And he couldn't respond to that. Not here. Not with Sarah's ghost hanging over him, and Zoe's secrets like inky shadows at their feet. Not with these kids who deserved better sneaking glances at him through the glass, already recognizing him.

He still wanted to be inside her more than was wise. More than was healthy. More than he was likely to be able to ignore. So he told himself that was why he was doing this. Because it was the only explanation that made any sense.

"How does this work?" he asked, and his voice was far hoarser that it should have been.

"Come here every day," she told him sharply, as if she knew what he was thinking. He believed she might. "Do what you can. Meet with my team every Tuesday for a status update." Her gray eyes met his, and he wished he was a different man. A better one. Some kind of good one, even. "Definitely do not mention *hate fucking* again. Just do as you're told, Mr. Grant, and we'll be fine."

Chapter Five

She was playing with fire.

But in the weeks that followed, Zoe convinced herself she knew what she was doing. That it was a controlled blaze. That she had it under control. That those strange things that had wound so tightly between them, dark and bright at once even in a high school hallway, were a figment of her imagination and anyway, weren't anything to worry about.

Which was a good thing, because Hunter was enough to worry about. Even—especially—when he was "behaving."

Zoe had spent a lot of time researching what the tabloids called The Hunter Effect. Now she got to watch it in action as he unleashed it in a relatively restrained way on the Manhattan social circuit, exactly as she'd planned.

"Must you smile like that at *every* woman who looks at you?" Zoe asked impatiently as she tried to keep from rolling her eyes at the logjam of admirers who all but cooed at him as he swaggered by in white tie at the annual Viennese Opera Ball to benefit Carnegie Hall, held in the distinctly elegant Waldorf Astoria. In a sea of resplendent creatures, he seemed to glow that little bit brighter—his notoriety be damned.

"That's how I smile, Zoe."

"You have several DEFCON levels of a smile and if you don't downgrade to a more manageable one right now, you'll cause a riot."

"I like riots."

"What a surprise. But we're going for restrained and under-the-radar elegance tonight, not a brawl. I know it's a stretch."

Hunter turned that riotous smile on her, then. It was a bone-melting, slumberous affair. Lazy blue eyes, that curve of his confident mouth, and that stunning physique dressed so beautifully it nearly made the photographers weep as they took his picture again and again. Zoe pretended that what shook inside her, hard and long, was simple hunger. She'd missed dinner.

"Put it away," she told him, and then let out a long-suffering sigh, as if he bored her.

She wished he did. More every day.

But even when he wasn't smiling so seductively, he was formidable. A force of personality and presence and, much as it pained her to admit it, breathtaking to watch in action. Zoe dragged him to a hospital to minister to terminal patients, where he spent two solid hours reading to a pair of little boys who gazed at him as if he hung a new moon with every word. She took him to a lunch to benefit libraries, where he so thoroughly charmed the dour, otherwise matronly librarians in question that he made them all blush and then giggle as those girls had in his gym that night when he'd been wearing much less.

"He's a bad, bad man," one of them told Zoe in an undertone, fanning herself theatrically.

"That is the literal truth," Zoe replied testily. She smiled, hoping that might play off her unprofessional show of pique, but the the other woman only laughed.

"It's that sparkle in his eyes," the librarian confided. "Like he wants you to be in on the joke. How can you help but forgive him everything?"

How indeed?

It raised the question: How had he managed to turn the entire country against him? Because the more time Zoe spent with him, the more she understood that his terrible reputation, his tantrums and his scandals, must all have been deliberate.

She even said as much on a snowy afternoon in Prospect Park out in Brooklyn, where Hunter "happened by" to build snowmen with a particularly photogenic group of schoolchildren.

"You can charm anyone you meet without even trying," she said flatly as they trudged back across the field, their boots crunching into the icy layer hidden beneath the fluffy new snow. "So why go to all the trouble to become so universally hated?"

"Total commitment," he said at once in that smirky way of his. "That's how I roll."

"I'm serious."

He wore a fleece hat tugged low on his forehead and a scarf pulled high around his neck, and that still failed to soften the impact of his bright gaze. It seared into her, warming her up from within, making her forget the cold, the snow, the long walk. Making her forget for a long, dizzying moment that she needed to keep this fire contained or it might destroy what was left of her.

Reminding her that so much of what she saw was an act and *this* Hunter, of the direct blue gaze and that surprisingly somber cast to his mouth, was more likely the real one.

God help her.

"A better question would be, given that I *am* so despised, how do you think these sappy photo ops of me in obviously staged poses with a hundred rosy-cheeked little cherubs is going to play?" he asked.

"Accidentally," she replied, and told herself she wasn't unnerved by all that sudden *focus*.

"I don't know what that means."

"You will. The good news is that I know exactly what it means."

He looked at her again, long and deep, and she wondered why she didn't incinerate on the spot, and who cared how cold it was? She thought for a moment he might say something else, and she braced herself. She didn't know why. There was something about the dark scrape of naked tree branches behind him, the gray sky above, the snow falling all around him like a message. Like something she didn't want to examine too closely. But he only shoved his hands into the pockets of his coat, bent his head against the wind and kept walking.

Zoe told herself that was a good thing. Because it was. Of course it was.

"I want you to take a carriage ride through Central Park," she announced early one morning at one of the coffee meetings she'd demanded.

Hunter glared at her, looking sleepy and cranky and ridiculously hot in jeans and a turtleneck sweater and that unshaven fighter's jaw of his.

"Let me guess. I burst into song at the first lamppost and we all turn into animation that can go viral on YouTube." He scowled at her, then at his coffee. "No, thank you."

"It wouldn't be a romantic date," Zoe continued as if he hadn't spoken. She sat across from him at a tiny wooden table that was too rickety and much too small. She pulled out her BlackBerry and made a show of looking at it, as if she wasn't entirely too aware of how *much* of the space he took up in their little corner of the café, of how big he was. How shockingly attractive, even when he clearly wasn't trying to be anything of the kind. Maybe especially then. She kept her tone bright. "You need to take your mother."

He let out a short, startled sort of laugh.

"Alison Blodgett Grant would no more ride around in a hired carriage like a common tourist than she would turn naked cartwheels down Broadway," Hunter said derisively. "Besides, she no longer takes my calls. She diverts them to her secretary, who vets them for potential upset before passing any messages along."

Zoe stopped pretending she was interested in her Black-Berry.

"Your mother has a secretary? I didn't think she worked."

"She has a social secretary and no, she doesn't work. Not the way you mean."

"But surely she—"

"Zoe." She'd never heard that tone of voice from him. It made her sit a little bit straighter—and go quiet. "My mother wanted a senator. Prestige and power and all those centuries of upper-crust breeding put to good use. She thinks sports are for children, not grown men. And she's appalled that any child of hers has appeared in the tabloids, much less as many times as I have. To say nothing of the many embarrassing scandals that landed me there, every one of which she views as a personal slap in the face." The smile that cracked over his lips then made Zoe's heart seem to squeeze tight. "She isn't going to race down to New York to save me from myself. I promise."

There was absolutely no reason in the world she should have to fight off the powerful urge to comfort him then. To put her hands on his, to touch him, to *do something* about the way he sat there, alone and resigned and not even aware, she thought, that he looked so terribly sad.

Get a hold of yourself, she snapped inside her head. *This is his act. It's all an act.*

But she didn't believe that.

"Your sister, then," she said instead, clearing her throat. "Nora?"

"Do you have more than one?" She knew he didn't.

"Nora has better things to do." He frowned down at his coffee, and it took him a long while to look up at her again. "Or so I assume. She's a very busy little socialite."

"She runs a fairly impressive art charity in SoHo, in fact," Zoe said. She frowned when he looked blank. "Did you not know that?"

"I knew it." He rubbed a hand over his sexily unshaven jaw, and it was insane that Zoe wanted to do that herself. That her palms actually itched to do it. She grabbed her too-hot mug of coffee, as punishment, and didn't let go when it hurt. "She's practically an infant."

"She's twenty-four."

"Exactly."

Zoe sighed. "You do realize that all those strippers you had flocking to you that morning were your sister's age? If not younger? Does it hurt to have such an extreme double standard, Mr. Grant?"

He took a long pull from his coffee then set it down, too carefully. And when his gaze swung to meet hers, it was fierce with temper and she shouldn't have cared.

"Leave my sister out of it," he said shortly. "She has enough to deal with as the living, breathing repository for all my mother's dynastic fantasies. And as for those strippers…" He leaned forward and Zoe found she was holding her breath. "For someone who spends the bulk of her time manipulating perception to serve her clients, you sure do believe what you see pretty easily." His voice was as dark and harsh as the way he looked at her. "It's a good thing you're hot, Zoe. Or you'd be nothing but a pain in the ass."

She concentrated on that last part—the offensive part— because she didn't want to know what he meant. She didn't want to feel anything but vague pity and rather more pointed disgust when she looked at him.

But she hadn't felt either of those things in a while. And it took exactly one phone call that afternoon to find out that Hunter hadn't been partying well into the morning the day she'd tracked him to that strip club. His very famously married ex-teammate had been the one out for an all-night party. Hunter had been called in by the wife when the man was still going strong the next morning, according to the club manager. He'd gathered up his friend, poured him into a car and then had paid for everything—including the strippers' time. With a very generous tip.

Almost as if he wasn't who she thought he was.

Daniel, of course, vehemently disagreed.

The rest of the team found their meetings with Hunter— which Zoe stopped attending after that last coffee, because she couldn't allow herself to lose sight of her goals, and all of that time with him seemed to lead straight to blindness— no more or less outrageous than the ones they had with the rest of their wealthy, entitled client base.

But not Daniel.

"He's a pig," Daniel snarled. He stood in front of her desk

in a fury, so angry Zoe didn't dare voice her confusing little thought—that she'd thought he was a pig when she'd met him, but hadn't in some time.

And didn't really like hearing him called that now, if she was honest.

"He's a client," she said instead. Daniel didn't need to know that Hunter hadn't sought her out and therefore wouldn't be paying for their services. No one needed to know that. "A very rich client. What does it matter if he's a pig?"

"You can tell your *client* that if he calls me weak and breakable again in that he-man way of his, I'll quit."

It was important that she not laugh, Zoe understood. That she keep her face absolutely clear of any amusement.

"Why did Hunter call you weak and breakable?" she asked, very carefully. "Was he threatening you?"

"He's a bully," Daniel snapped. "That's what bullies *do*. And the fact he's managed to snow you doesn't mean it works on anyone else, Zoe. He's a disaster waiting to happen. Why can't you see that?"

"I know what I'm doing, Daniel," she retorted, with a little more heat than she should have. Daniel looked as if she'd slapped him, and Zoe didn't feel as guilty about that as she should have, either. "Listen," she said in a much calmer tone. "You have to trust me. You always have before."

"I trust you," he muttered, though she could see he was still angry.

But the trouble was, she wasn't sure she trusted herself.

Because when she was with Hunter, she sometimes forgot that the purpose of all of this was revenge.

Hunter rang the bell of the latter-day speakeasy in Chelsea that night, at precisely nine-thirty as ordered, and let the staff member lead him through the lush interior. It was a plush and sexy expanse of velvet and wood, debonair comfort accented by ambitious cocktails and mood lighting. He was delivered to a private seating area surrounded by gauzy, romantic curtains, through which he could glimpse only the faintest suggestion of the person he assumed was Zoe.

"When you demanded I meet you here I didn't realize it was a bordello," he said as he pushed his way through the shimmering barrier like the bull in a china shop he was. "I would have dressed more appropriately. In my belly dancing costume, for example. You may not know this about me, Zoe, but I do a mean dance of the seven veils."

And then Hunter stopped in his tracks, taking his first really good look at the rest of her without those filmy curtains in the way. It was like getting decisively and comprehensively sacked by an entire, and very large, defensive line.

"Don't get too excited," Zoe said coolly, her chin rising.

He couldn't help himself. It was that slick parody of a dress in one of the dark gray shades she favored, clinging to every curve and hollow, plane and stretch of her perfectly toned figure. It made his mouth go dry and his head swim around in loopy circles, all the blood in his body surging toward the most irreverent and unmanageable part of him.

"I don't get excited," he drawled, in an approximation of his usual careless self, the guy who was bored by everything. He remembered that guy. He'd been him all of five seconds ago. "Did you forget? I'm rich, handsome and notorious. People are generally excited to see *me*."

"If you say so," she replied, predictably dismissive, which, also predictably, made him want her all the more. "Positive attention isn't the same thing as negative attention, you know. Unless you're an attention whore."

"I'm whatever kind of whore you want me to be, Zoe," he said, grinning when her lips thinned. "Have you reconsidered your position on a good, dirty, head-clearing hate fuck? Because I haven't. For the record."

That cool gray gaze of hers was reproachful, but he imagined he saw the hint of heat in the depths of it.

"I had an earlier meeting that required more formal attire. I didn't dress for you." She looked marginally agitated, and he congratulated himself on even so small a crack in the Zoe Brook armor. "You're looking at me as if we're on a date. We're not."

"You're a destroyer of dreams, Zoe. A killjoy of the highest order. Does it give you pleasure to ruin everything you touch?"

"Besides," she continued, eyeing him in that regal way of hers, a look only slightly marred by the faintest twitch of her lips, "it would serve no practical or strategic purpose for you to be seen on a date with me. We need to find you a social worker. Maybe a kindergarten teacher. Someone sweet and wholesome and good."

"That sounds thrilling. Truly."

"Her virtuous love will make you a better man."

"I doubt that very much."

"That's the point of virtue. It can be harnessed and utilized. Everyone believes that love—especially saintly and wholesome love—inspires change. So does religion, but that's a harder sell, and it requires you carry on about God in public places. Squeaky-clean, rehabilitating love it is."

"I didn't realize you ran a dating service." He kept his own voice mild. "Don't I get to fill out a detailed questionnaire discussing my various sexual preferences? To start, I like my women obedient and adventurous."

"Do those things usually go hand in hand?"

"Want me to show you?" He smiled when she only rolled her eyes. "That's a pity. But I'm sure there are some wild and horny preschool teachers out there, aren't there, stuffed full of their own virtue and gagging to take a little direction from a man like me?"

But Hunter wasn't thinking too hard about the secret, naughty lives of teachers, because he was caught in the epic expanse of Zoe's gloriously sculpted legs, in the way she shifted against the banquette seat, crossing those perfect legs at the knee and making him forget his own name. All that skin, daringly bared to the winter elements outside, a rich ivory cream all the way down to another pair of impossible shoes, those brash ankle boots that made him think of punk rock and the kind of edgy, demanding sex that wrecked whole lives.

The kind he would have with her, sooner or later. Or he might die from wanting her like this.

And then there was the rest of her hot, trim body in that scandalous lick of smoke, with only a single, almost poignant diamond at her throat, her black hair piled high in something that looked complicated and graceful, and made him want to sink his hands and his teeth deep into it—into her—

Maybe she wasn't beautiful. Maybe she was something far more intense that that. Maybe *beautiful* was insipid next to Zoe Brook and what she could do with a simple strapless sheath of a dress.

What she was doing to him. Right now.

"Sit down, Mr. Grant," she ordered him, her frown looking more annoyed than truly bothered, which was, he understood, yet another slap meant to put him in his place. He liked it.

"Stop calling me that," he said. "It makes me want to demonstrate that we're on far less formal footing, or should be. Is that what you want?"

Her lips pressed together and if he wasn't mistaken, that was a glimmer of amusement in her blue-gray gaze. She only nodded slightly, after a moment, awarding him the point.

But a win was a win. And the victory, however minor, washed through him like heat. Like whiskey.

Like sex.

"Say it," he ordered her.

"I beg your pardon?"

"Say it," he said again, and rougher. "My name."

He couldn't read the expression he saw on her face then. The glitter in her wild, dangerous eyes. But he could feel the tension in his own body and knew this was much more important to him than it should have been. Very much like this—like she—was more than merely a scorching-hot woman in a scandalous dress.

Like she was the only thing keeping him alive. The only thing that could.

He didn't want to think about that. He wanted his name in her mouth. He wanted to hear it.

"If I say your name, will you stop hovering over me?" She sounded cross, exasperated, but he could see something else in those stormy winter eyes. Maybe what he wanted to see. Maybe the truth. "You're making me anxious."

"If you say my name, I'll give you anything you want."

"Fine." But she held out another beat, then another. She swallowed. Then surrendered. *"Hunter."*

"Was that so hard?" he asked, amused. "You didn't fall apart. It's only a name."

He took his time sitting down, savoring this moment. First he shrugged out of his coat, tossing it aside carelessly, not taking his eyes off her. Then he settled himself down much too close to her, almost on top of her, grinning when she hissed in an annoyed breath. She went stiff and straight, and he relaxed, stretching his arm out on the high back, a single, easy crook of his elbow away from holding her in his embrace.

"You really enjoy invading the personal space of others, don't you?" she asked frostily. But she didn't move away.

"I'm a big guy." He breathed in the sleek and expensive scent she wore, which wasn't half as alluring as that hint of lavender he'd smelled on her skin before. "I can't help it if I take up a lot of space."

"You use your body as a weapon," she retorted.

He took his time looking her over. Memorizing her, as if he wasn't sure he'd get to be this close to her again. To that perfect, clever arch of her dark brows. To that stubborn, too-smart mouth, glossy tonight in the dim, flickering light. He could see her pulse catapult against the soft skin at her neck, telling him exactly what it cost her to sit this close to him. And yet she made no attempt to pull away, not even when his gaze moved even lower, until he nearly forgot himself completely in the tempting hollow between her breasts.

He wanted to taste her again more than he wanted his next breath. He had no idea how he held himself back— except he wanted her to want him, too. He wanted her to feel as outside her own skin as he did. As undone by this attraction.

This...*thing* that was gradually taking him over. What was left of him.

He nodded toward that smoky sin of a dress.

"Pot," he said, then he indicated himself with a jerk of his hand. "Kettle."

She regarded him for a long moment, that heady mix of awareness and wariness in her gaze. "I don't know what you mean."

"It's a coincidence, then, that you happen to be wearing a dress that may in fact be painted directly on to your skin tonight. For your 'meeting' in this notably noncorporate environment, with a client you blackmailed into working with you. A client who knows what your inner thighs feel like beneath his hands. Not to mention how you taste." He laughed. "I'm sure the fact you look edible played no part at all in your decision to wear it tonight."

"It isn't for you." Her voice was lofty.

"You can't use your body the way you do, Zoe, and then cry foul if others do the same."

"I'm not an oversize man, all bulky muscles and caveman strength, lumbering through the world like a flatfooted thug."

"Neither am I," Hunter said, surprised to find he was grinning. "My feet have an adorable arch. Everybody says so. Want to see?"

"You're impossible," she muttered, but he imagined he saw the slightest quirk in the corner of her mouth, like a laugh bitten back before it betrayed her. "And I don't want to talk about your innumerable body flaws. I want to talk about your behavior toward my associates."

"I'm suddenly significantly less interested in this conversation."

"You can't antagonize Daniel," Zoe told him sternly. "You may not realize it, but you need him. Calling him names isn't smart."

"David is a punk," Hunter said dismissively.

"His name is *Daniel*."

"I don't care what his name is." Though he knew it, of course. He eyed her. "He's in love with you."

She didn't deny it. "That's one more thing that's absolutely none of your business."

"You're not dating him, or you'd defend him. You'd tell me to go fuck myself."

"I might tell you that anyway," she retorted. "No matter who I'm dating." She showed him that little smirk, and he felt it in his groin, as if she'd leaned over and licked the length of him there and then. He felt himself go hard like stone. Hot. But she was still talking. "I don't know what it is about you that brings out the intense desire to do you harm. But then, I'm sure you get that all the time."

"I'm an acquired taste," he agreed.

"That most people spit out?" That arched brow, that clever twist of her mouth.

"I prefer it when they swallow," he said, his gaze hot on those glossy, glossy lips of hers. "But I'm not going to lie, Zoe. I'm not very picky."

She tilted back her head—to throw something else at him, he was certain, and he found himself readying for it, all the adrenaline and focus he'd used on the field trained on her instead—but, impossibly, she giggled.

Then jerked against the seat as if electrified, clapping her hands over her mouth as if she wanted to stuff that incongruously girlish sound straight back in it, her eyes snapping to his in a mix of astonishment and horror.

He loved it.

"See?" His grin was too big, taking over his face, moving in him in a way that felt like sunlight. "You like me."

She shook her head, a firm denial, but her hands still covered her mouth as if it would betray her otherwise, and he didn't recognize that buoyant feeling that swelled in him then. Light and shiny. Bright.

"For some reason, no one believes this," he confided. "But I'm incredibly likeable."

Zoe dropped her hands, but she was smiling as if she couldn't help herself, and it killed him. It pierced him straight through. It knocked down walls he'd erected so long ago, he wasn't sure he knew what they were for—and more of that sunlight poured through him, rolled in him, made him forget, for a moment, who he was. What he was. What shadows lurked in him.

What he'd done. What he hadn't.

Zoe coughed. "I'm certain I was laughing—"

"Giggling, to be precise."

"—*at* you, Hunter. Not with you."

"I don't think so."

And he was laughing, too, realizing how close he was

to her, how her head was tipped back so her hair brushed against his arm. Her gray eyes had gone bluer than he'd ever seen them, and that pooled in him, making his stomach knot and those shadows that lived in all his empty places seem even brighter, somehow. He didn't know what the hell that meant.

He traced a vague pattern down the side of her lovely face with a lazy finger, skirting that razor-sharp, dangerous mouth, which only made him want her more. And he felt that white-hot heat flare between them again, tighter this time. Tauter. Winching them together, making it hurt.

"Who else knows the fierce Zoe Brook snorts a little bit when she giggles like a schoolgirl?" he asked softly. "I imagine that's proprietary information. Don't worry, I won't tell anyone. I want it for myself."

He watched her pull in a breath as if her life depended on it. Or as if his might—that and the heat in her gaze, bright and unmistakable. It lit him up all over again, brushfires building into blazes. Walls crumbling into ash.

"Since when are you sweet?" she whispered, her voice rough. The need in it damning them both.

"Never." But his fingers still drew lazy symbols on the satin expanse of her cheek, her neck.

"This is sweet." Her voice was stronger then, and rang with accusation. There was that hint of a frown on her face, etched between her brows. "You can't deny it."

"If I'm doing it," he said, and he could hear the fire in

his voice, the desire, "it can't be anything like sweet. By definition. You can ask any of my eight million enemies. Or read their depositions."

"Sweet is unacceptable."

"Just wait a few moments," he assured her, too many things he didn't want to accept in his own voice then, the low grit of it, the urgency at such odds with the reverent way he learned the shape of her, each clever eyebrow, with his fingertips. "I'm sure I'll turn back into an asshole. I can't help myself."

He watched, fascinated, as emotions he didn't understand rose and fell across the face she normally kept so cool. He only recognized the flash of panic, followed quickly by a kind of resignation that made his chest ache.

"I only know how to break things," he said gruffly, suddenly, and he saw her react to that, as if it hurt her. "Zoe, I don't want—"

She didn't let him finish. Her gray eyes went dark—too dark—and then she surged forward, a liquid twist of her perfect body, her hands coming up to frame his face. To hold him steady, as if she had the power to immobilize him that easily.

But then—he realized with some surprise as he simply sat there, his own hands circling her wrists but not attempting to shift her grip on him at all—it turned out that she did.

He tried again. "Zoe—"

"Shut up," she ordered him. He heard the fire and the

panic, the madness and the need, and he felt it all inside him, rising like a tide. "For God's sake, Hunter. *Just shut up.*"

And then she closed the final bit of that searing, electric space between them and slammed her mouth to his.

Chapter Six

Zoe kissed him as if her life depended on it.

All that fire. All that danger, that impossible need. All the things she felt that she shouldn't, that until him she'd thought she *couldn't*. That wildfire, burning through her, through him, making her shake against him as she tasted that mouth of his, again and again.

Because she thought that maybe her life did depend on this, after all.

Zoe had already showed him too much. She didn't understand how it had happened. This wasn't supposed to be complicated. *He* wasn't.

But she'd finally realized that there was only one way to deal with Hunter Grant.

He thought he wanted her? Then he could have her— but only on her terms. She thought there was a certain poetry in taking back from this man what other men had taken from her.

He'd said he'd crawl. She'd make sure he did.

But first, she kissed him. She took charge, and she took

what she wanted from that too-clever mouth of his that shouldn't have attracted her, much less beguiled her. She shifted over him, shimmying the tight column of her dress up her thighs so she could climb over his lap. He made a deep, guttural sound that should have been surrender, but instead echoed in her like a battle cry.

Because it was.

Zoe was fighting for her life with every slide of his perfect mouth on hers, every shift of his stunning athlete's body beneath her. She pressed herself closer to him, angling her head to taste him deeper, wetter, hotter. She found the thick ridge of his need and rode it.

She would do the taking. She would take what she wanted and leave him behind when she was done. She would conquer this thing. She would win, at last.

But it didn't help that he tasted like fire.

He kissed her as if she was a revelation and he was a connoisseur who trafficked in such things. He licked into her, tasting her and tantalizing her in equal measure, making the flames dance, the fire burn hotter, wild and impossible. He was hard between her legs, packed muscle and all of that delicious male power, but he didn't use any of it against her.

It made her shake. It made her *want*. It made her forget what she was doing—

He was the one who pulled back, and she hated it. Hated that he had the presence of mind when she was still so lost. Hated that he looked at her for a long, breathless moment, still so hard against her, his bright eyes seeming to pierce right through her. Hated that all she wanted—with every shuddering beat of her heart, with every harsh breath—was his mouth on hers again.

"You taste too good," he rasped out, one of his hands moving, his thumb rubbing over her lips, branding them with so simple a touch. She felt it in her breasts, heavy against the tight bodice of her dress. She felt it deep inside her, hungry and throbbing and pressed against him.

His eyes were too blue. As if he was some kind of sun, lighting them both up, though she knew that was impossible. He was too debauched and she was too damaged. None of this was real. None of this could be happening.

But he shifted beneath her, one of his big hands wrapping over her hip and holding her to him, and she stopped telling herself what was or wasn't real. Because she felt him everywhere.

"How can you taste so good?"

His voice was no more than a murmur, then, as if he was crooning it to her, and she wanted to tell him he was wrong—that she was blackened within and ruined for years now—but he didn't wait for her answer. He reared up and captured her mouth with his again, turning her inside out.

And Zoe melted. And she forgot.

She forgot what she'd been through, what she'd survived.

Who she'd become. Who she'd created from the wreckage of her former self.

It was as if he kissed the Zoe she might have been, longing and magic and all those bold, bright futures. A tumult of color. A cacophony of possibility.

And all that delicious, drugging heat.

And for a moment, Zoe gave in to that insanity, as if toppling through the back of a wardrobe or down a rabbit hole. She let herself go.

She let him taste her. Tempt her. As if they were other people. As if they could do this without paying for it later when she knew full well they couldn't.

There was always a price.

But for a little while, with his mouth like a searing, addicting flame against hers, she pretended otherwise. She pretended she didn't know better. She pretended there was nothing at all but him. This kiss. This frantic heat, the way she rocked against him and made them both sigh. The fire that shouldn't have existed in the first place.

Nothing at all but him.

God help her, but she couldn't seem to stop.

"Your place," she said then, tearing her mouth from his.

He blinked up at her, his hands gripping her bottom, holding her in a way that might get them arrested should a staff member stick his or her head through the gauzy curtains of their little nook.

"What?" His voice was thick.

"You want to fuck me, don't you?" Her throat was harsh with all that longing, and her determination to keep from sobbing out her need.

She could control this. She *would* control this.

He blinked, and his clear eyes became unreadable again. "Is that a trick question?"

"I'd prefer not to attract the attention of local law enforcement," she said coolly, moving back and up in a single sleek movement. She held his gaze as she smoothed her dress back into place. "So. Your place?"

It was only sex. And it was the only way she was going to break this spell.

She couldn't risk letting him chase her any further. He was too intuitive, shockingly. He saw too much. She had to stop being surprised by that, and start taking the appropriate steps to counter it.

All she had to do was let him catch her. He'd be bored before he pulled out, the way he always was with all his little starlets and models-slash-actresses the tabloids tallied up each year, and this taut little dance of theirs would be over.

She could hide again—and stay hidden. And then she could use him the way she'd planned she would, to help take Jason Treffen down, with none of this extraneous *heat*.

All she had to do was survive the night.

"Well?" she asked. It was a taunt. A dare. "Don't tell me, after all this, that you're nothing but a tease. I'll be devastated."

"Oh," he said softly, a hint of sensual menace in his tone, "I'm not a tease."

"Is this not romantic enough for you?" She smirked at him. "Do you need a card? Some flowers?"

She didn't understand that smile he gave her then, heart-stopping and intense. Just as she didn't understand the way her breath caught when he stood.

"It never hurts," he said, his voice low, as if he was talking about something else. As if this was a line or two of poetry and he was reciting it to win her favor. "I enjoy gardenias. And the occasional sunflower, but only in moderation. They're so gaudy."

The way he looked at her then, at her breasts and her belly, at her legs and then back again, hurt. It all hurt. She felt raw. Undone.

But she knew she had to do this.

So when he extended his hand with an oddly taut sort of look in his eyes and a kind of fierceness in his expression as he looked down at her, as if he was holding himself back from taking her right there where they stood, Zoe told herself this was the only way—*it was*—and took it.

She strode into Hunter's immense apartment, staring imperiously around her as if she wasn't the least bit impressed by its three vast levels so high above Wall Street, its spiral stairs, stunningly high white walls and dizzying views showing lower Manhattan in every direction.

Zoe stopped in the middle of the sunken, sterile living space, pivoting around in a circle as she unbuttoned the dramatic, thickly lined cape she'd worn against the winter cold. She eyed the gargantuan television set flat against one wall, the crisp corners of the scrupulously modern sectional that could have seated Hunter's entire previous football team, and the total lack of anything even hinting at Hunter's personality.

No photographs. No books. No art to relieve the white sheen of the walls. Not even the collection of trophies and sports memorabilia she would have imagined must be ubiquitous for a man with his résumé. No pulse. A robot could have lived here. Maybe this was who Hunter really was, she told herself: empty and barren. Nothing more than a very expensive, very chilly shell.

She didn't know why everything inside her rebelled at the thought—but it was time to lock such unhelpful thoughts away and do what she must.

"It looks like you live in a morgue," she said, tossing her cape onto the sofa with flourish. Her dark, inky blue cape was the only splash of color in the entire, sprawling penthouse, and it made her feel edgy. Some kind of restless, as if that simple fact—as if all of this—held meaning she was afraid to look at too closely.

"You should think about livening it up a bit," she continued when he didn't speak. "Nothing too crazy, mind you. Maybe a single, solitary painting to relieve the hospital-meets–serial-killer atmosphere you have going on?"

She looked over at Hunter then, and her heart kicked at her, then started to gallop in her chest.

He still didn't speak. He only watched her, his blue eyes darker than they should have been, darker than was possible, gleaming so brightly she nearly forgot the lack of color everywhere else. He shrugged out of his coat, letting it drop where he stood, though it didn't strike her as carelessness. It struck her as *intention*.

He didn't move that electric blue gaze from her. She wasn't sure he so much as blinked.

It was unnerving.

It moved over her, inside her, like a blast of near-painful heat.

"Or perhaps that's what you like," she said, as if nothing about him got beneath her skin. As if she was utterly unmoved as she stood there, her hands on her hips and her head at an arrogant tilt, staring back at him. As if this wasn't a skirmish that she absolutely had to win, no matter what it took from her. "Do you like to play doctor, Hunter? Is that what this is? A little operating-room style to make you feel sexy?"

His sculpted lips moved then into something far too intense to be a smile, and she fought off a shiver, remembering how they felt against hers. She thought he might say something, but he merely indicated the spiral staircase nearest her with a peremptory jerk of that iron jaw of his.

"I thought you'd never shut up in that bar," she continued coolly, aware she was poking at him, trying to shatter the tension that had her in its grip before it ripped her in two. "And now you've gone completely silent? I don't know whether to be amused or alarmed."

"Either one works for me."

It was a starkly male rasp of sound, scraping against her skin, insinuating itself into her blood, the very beat of her heart. The air in the cavernous apartment thinned. Then blistered.

So did she.

Zoe decided there was nothing to do but keep playing her part, and hope it would work. Because it had to work.

Because there was absolutely no way she could risk herself like this again.

She crossed the room slowly, making sure her hips rolled, making sure she used every part of her body as she moved.

An invitation. A challenge. The perfect male fantasy.

Sensual and powerful at once, the way she wanted this to be—the way *she* wanted to be. She watched his blue eyes narrow, watched the skin pull taut over his inhumanly beautiful cheekbones.

Desire. Need.

She told herself it didn't matter how dry her throat was, or that the wild galloping beat in her chest set her on the razor's edge of panic. It didn't matter that she could feel the way he looked at her in the wet heat between her legs, in the wild flush that suffused her skin, in the aching stiffness of her nipples, in every ragged-edged breath she tried to keep him from hearing. What mattered was that she make Hunter lose *his* control.

She could do this. She could.

His eyes were too bright on hers, his gaze too hard, and once again, he saw things he shouldn't. "Change your mind?"

Zoe made herself laugh, told herself the butterflies in her

stomach were nothing more or less than nerves. He might have made her feel something in her office that day, in the bar during that wild kiss, in all the strange moments they'd spent together in these odd winter weeks, but that would pass. And then there would simply be getting through the night intact, so she could take charge of him again, of this, of the revenge plot she'd started hatching since before she'd escaped from Treffen, Smith, and Howell.

"Did you?" she shot back.

"That's not going to happen," he said, and then that smile of his went feral.

He nodded toward the stairs again. Zoe fought to keep from shaking, at least where he might see it, and forced herself to turn toward the metal spiral that rose elegantly from this floor all the way up to the top of the three levels.

Calm and easy, she chanted at herself. *Be casual, yet in control. As if you do this all the time. Or at all.*

Zoe climbed his stairs slowly, aware of him behind her the moment she began, like a wall of heat. A scalding furnace of male fire—and he wasn't even touching her. She hoped he couldn't see the shiver of gooseflesh that rose on her arms, her neck—but she heard him make the slightest, smallest sound, deep and low and satisfied, and she knew that he had.

He knew. Men like him always knew. It was what made him a predator, the kind she could feel deep in her bones, like an ache from within, as if he was using her against herself.

When she reached the second level, she shifted slightly to look over her shoulder, and he grinned at her.

Hot and certain. Fallen angels and a thousand sins in that searing blue gaze, and she felt it like a blow. Like a lick of fire, trailing from her shoes up the length of her spine, burning her alive where she stood.

"Keep going," he said in that same low, growly way, that made her body clench and then flood with more of that exquisite heat.

He was a few steps below, one hand on the rail and one hand braced against the stair above his head, and she had the dizzying notion that he was doing that deliberately—to keep his hands off her.

For now.

As if he wasn't sure he could control himself if he didn't.

Zoe turned away from him and swallowed hard against her pounding pulse, her growing inability to breathe. Her limbs felt heavy, weighed down with that same fire, and she wanted nothing more than to simply let herself burn.

Instead, she kept moving. She kicked off one ankle boot, then the next, smirking at the greedy sound he made when she did.

"Everyone likes a Cinderella fantasy," she murmured. "Even the most hated man in New York, it seems."

"Does that make me—?"

"Prince Charming? Hardly."

"I'm remarkably charming. Nine out of ten tabloids agree."

"I've seen absolutely no evidence to support that."

"Would you like me to prove to you how charming I am?" His voice was smooth and closer than it should have been, his breath fanning against her ear, the exposed skin at her neck, and she had to fight to keep from shivering. From melting. From surrendering then and there. "All you have to do is reach behind you, and I'll charm you all you like."

Zoe laughed, amazed it came out so throaty, so full. Sex and desire, right there in the sound, as naked as if she was helpless beneath him, spread open to his touch. As powerful as if she knew what she was doing with this, with him, with this pointed flirtation that could end only one way.

It was almost as if she was doing this simply because she wanted to do it. As if she really did want him this much.

The novelty of that crazy notion made her sway on her feet and, deeply off-balance, she went with it, holding on to the rail for support as she turned to look down at him again, now only a single step behind her. Big and hard and blocking her retreat.

Weakness was bad, she told herself, no matter what kind. It shouldn't feel so good, so deliciously feminine, as if *this* kind of breathlessness was a good thing. Hot. Encompassing. As if she might never breathe fully again, thank God.

"There are better uses for you than shoe retrieval, I think." She told herself she was *trying* to sound like that, sexy and alluring. That it wasn't simply how she sounded when he was this close to her, making all her senses go haywire.

He smiled, and it was edged with a dark intent she felt

against her skin, sensual and stark, then deep inside, like a harder, deeper ache. The air around them—between them—felt thick. Sultry. Humid with this need, this pulsing desire, that made her feel real. *Real.* Flesh and blood, filled with yearning and capable of longing, like anyone else. That was what he did to her.

That might be the death of her.

Then again, that traitorous part of her whispered, *dying might be a small price to pay. Hunter might be worth it.*

It didn't matter what she felt, she reminded herself fiercely then, astonished at herself. It mattered what *he* felt, and she had to be prepared to manipulate that—and to handle it when he forgot her the moment he turned over and went to sleep. To use that.

This was all part of the plan.

"Unzip me," she ordered him then, presenting him with the hidden zipper at her side by lifting one arm up over her head, very slowly, with a deliberately sinuous grace designed to make him as wild as she felt.

She thought he froze for a second, but she must have imagined it, because when he reached for her, his hands were as steady as all those dark promises in his deep blue gaze. The feel of his hands against her was a torture, a gift. She forced herself not to react when his fingers brushed gently over the skin he exposed as he tugged her zipper down to her hip, though deep inside, she cracked and shattered.

Soon there'd be nothing left of her but rubble.

But she could hide that, she knew. She could hide anything.

"Thank you," she said with a deep calm she didn't feel at all. "Remember when you promised to be my willing slave? Now's your chance to prove it."

That smile of his went wolfish and her breath deserted her in a rush.

"Keep walking," he said, "and I'll prove any number of things."

She believed him.

Zoe turned away, panic mixing with that terrible excitement inside her.

She started up the stairs again, but something had changed. Everything felt brittle, now. Taut. Fragile. Or she did. She ignored it all resolutely, gritting her teeth and peeling her dress down as she climbed. Inch by inch she took it off, slowly revealing herself to him as she took the last curve of the spiral that delivered her directly into the master bedroom that sprawled across the entire top level of the penthouse.

Where she couldn't help herself. She stopped dead.

It was like a chapel. The room was three sides glass and a huge steeple of even more glass above, arching up high over the dark wood floors and the central altar at the heart of it: his bed. It sat on a black dais raised a farther three wide steps up from the floor, massive and commanding, sleek and somehow primitively masculine all at once.

There was nothing else. There was only that carnal bed

and the crisp winter night on all sides, *just there* on the other side of the glass, making her feel almost as if she had vertigo—as if she'd tipped over the side of the world and was free-falling straight out into the sky.

Zoe thought wildly of cavemen and their pallets, wolves and their dens, as if Hunter really had dragged her off by her hair to this place, where the only color at all was on that bed, a pile of rich browns and deep reds that made her think of furs. Of sex and unwavering, irrevocable possession. Of the kind of brands that didn't mark the skin, but left scars all the same. Of a thousand things she shouldn't—didn't—want.

Of course she didn't.

But deep inside her, she felt shivery and too hot, a trembling and a liquid kind of weakness. The urge—the need—to simply spread herself out before him like a sacrifice to whatever ancient, unknowable deity it was who commanded this stark room, who understood the things that moved in her. That yearning to surrender and the longing to let go, to submit to whatever he might do to her however he might do it because she'd like it, too. That unprecedented desire to *give in,* at last, as if that meant safety instead of unbearable risk.

She wasn't afraid of him, she realized in a blinding flash of painful, shocking insight. She was afraid of *herself.* She was terrified of the things she wanted, that she'd never known she could want until right now.

But this wasn't about *want.* It was about revenge.

"Your groupies must love this room," she said, to remind herself of reality. Who he was, what this was.

He laughed, a low rumble of sound that she felt like a caress. "The groupies don't make it past the first floor. I have *some* standards."

Zoe let her dress fall to her feet before she could think better of it—and because she didn't want to think about the implications of what he'd said. She kicked the dress aside, moving briskly toward that huge, staggeringly male bed, pretending with all her might that it didn't get to her. That it was simply a bed.

That he was only a man.

This is only one night, she reminded herself. A handful of hours, at most, even if Hunter hadn't kissed her in that bar like a man who would rush through this, or anything else. *Anyone could handle one night.*

She knew that better than most.

"I suppose this will do," she said then, her voice clipped. Strained with all her false courage. She tried to wrench back the control she'd claimed she wanted so badly, thinking that might at least contain some of the damage. "Let me tell you how this works. I think I'll have you start on your knees again, facing the—"

"Zoe."

She didn't want to stop, but she did. She didn't want to turn to face him, but she did that, too. She had to do it. She had to prove he wasn't getting to her. She had to make sure he knew exactly how little this was affecting her—

But when she looked at him, it was like a blow. Hard and swift. Ruthless. She swayed on her feet again and for a terrifying moment thought she might actually topple over—but she caught herself.

Hunter looked like a stranger. Or more like himself, perhaps, than he'd been in all the time she'd known him, which made that terrifying longing creep through her again, then spread out, taking root deep inside. He was so powerful, so *male*. Strong and sure and focused on her with that brilliant, consuming heat. The city on the other side of that expanse of glass, the lights and bridges stretching out in all directions, swirled away and became part of that fire in his gaze, stamped hard on his face.

It occurred to her that she was as good as naked—worse than naked, really. She knew exactly what she looked like, standing there in nothing at all but two strips of provocative black lace. The strapless bra above and a pair of saucy boy shorts below that, despite their name, were entirely and decidedly feminine.

He'd been right when he'd accused her of using her body as a weapon. She'd honed hers to lethal perfection deliberately. She knew exactly how to package it, how to aim it, to get what she wanted.

If only he wasn't looking at her as if he held all the ammunition.

"I want—" she began, but everything was too hot. Behind her eyes, in that uncontrollable shaking in her knees, in that fever that had taken over her belly, her sex, shooting sensation into her fingers until they clenched on the need to touch him.

Hunter prowled toward her, sleekly male and not entirely tame and possibly the most glorious creature she'd ever beheld. He never took his eyes from hers. He never broke.

And Zoe had never felt more like prey in all her life.

Or more beautiful.

"Hunter..." she whispered.

His mouth looked hard and demanding as it crooked to one side. And his name sounded in the too-hot air between them like an invocation to that terrible god of his that would, she knew, destroy whatever was left of her.

She knew she should care about that. That it should make her run the way she had in her office that day. But she didn't move.

He closed the distance between them, then took her upper arms in his tough hands, hauling her to him. He wasn't gentle, and despite herself, despite that desperate part of her that knew better than to let this happen, it thrilled her.

Her breasts pressed against the planes of his impressive chest. *At last.* Her belly was soft against the unmistakable jut of his arousal. *Finally.* And he was built so big, so strong, all those heavy muscles and smooth, hard planes, like a fantasy of a man made real. He surrounded her.

He's seducing you, that treacherous voice whispered.

Zoe tipped her head back and reminded herself that she couldn't let this happen. Not like this, not all on his terms.

That the price she'd have to pay wasn't worth whatever brief moments of fire and awe she might—

"I have an idea," he said, in that guttural way of his that felt like another punch, directly into the center of her need. Shock waves vibrated out, teasing her aching nipples, making her breasts feel heavier. Making her skin prickle, too hot and too tight. "How about you stop playing these stupid games?"

"I'm not playing!" None of this felt even a little bit like *playing*.

"I appreciate the noble sacrifice of your lush little body to my savage needs," he said, and though his voice was still low, she heard that dark amusement in it that, even now, sparked in her. "But I want you needy, too. I want it real." His fingers flexed against her shoulders. It showered her in dancing flames and lightning bolts, and she trembled. He nodded. "I want *this*."

"No, you don't." Her voice was bitter then. Hardly hers at all. Pouring straight out of her past, and she couldn't seem to do a single thing to stop it.

He took one hand to her face, cradling her cheek in a manner she might have called tender, had that been possible. As it wasn't, she concentrated instead on the heat of it. The singe, the burn. *Hunter.*

"I insist on it," he said softly.

"Men prefer fantasy. No matter what. No matter what contortions of reality are required to make it work." She felt outside herself, then. Harsh and out of control. "It's the only thing you know how to do."

"Zoe."

She could have handled another command. But not her name, not like that, breathed out like a prayer. As if he'd heard that roughness behind her words, sensed the prick of tears behind her eyes. As if he knew the dark and terrible things in her she'd never share, not with anyone.

If anything should have made her bolt for the door, it was that. And yet she only stood, his hand cupping her cheek, his spectacular body pressed to hers, staring up at him as if this was something more than a means to an end.

"Let's get naked," he suggested, that gleam in his blue gaze turning molten, setting her ablaze, and she couldn't bring herself to fight how deep it went, how dangerous it was, how she thought it might be breaking her apart in ways she didn't know how to fix. "And see what happens."

He didn't wait for an answer; he simply picked her up. He settled her legs around his waist and took her mouth with his, one hand at the back of her head, the other hard on her bottom.

He was demanding. Untamed.

And that shock of electricity and a kind of primitive recognition she didn't want to acknowledge resonated inside her, catapulting her out of her head and the past at last—and directly into the fire.

His fire.

And Zoe let herself burn.

★ ★ ★

Yes, Hunter thought, and took her.

Her mouth, hot and sweet, clever and sharp and *his,* like the finest wine he'd ever tasted. His hands in her hair, tumbling the black silken mess of it down from the elegant twist that hid it away. That wild spice of her desire against his tongue, her tight curves wrapped around his body, incandescent and addictive—

Yes.

He felt as if he'd wanted her forever. As if he'd never wanted anything but this and never would. Zoe, her wicked mouth meeting his, daring him, challenging him even now.

And he couldn't get enough. He couldn't taste her enough, he couldn't get close enough. Finally, he wasn't frozen. He wasn't numb. He felt everything and he wanted more. *He wanted.*

Again and again, until they were both sated.

Yes.

She laughed then, a husky, inflamed sound, and he realized he'd spoken out loud.

But it penetrated that tight fist of need that held him in a vise. Hunter set her down on her feet, then smiled, and he could feel the edge in it. He saw her dark gray eyes widen slightly, heard her breath come harder.

Perhaps a better man wouldn't revel in that. But he did.

He moved toward her, backing her up, herding her toward the absurd monstrosity of a bed that dominated the room. Zoe swallowed convulsively, audibly, but she went. Slowly. Never taking her eyes from his.

He liked that, too.

Hunter pulled his shirt off with one hand, impatient with the split second he lost sight of her beneath the fabric. He reached down and unbuttoned his trousers, then forgot about them, because they'd reached the first step that led to his bed.

"Don't trip," he said, and his voice sounded like a stranger's in the thick silence. Rough and hot.

"Don't let me fall," she retorted, a flash of her usual fire moving over those flushed cheeks of hers, and Hunter grinned.

She was his. All of her. At last.

No masks. Only Zoe.

He didn't think he'd ever let her go.

"I'll pick you right back up again," he told her, and it should have alarmed him, how deeply he meant that. How far it went. But her eyes were like the sea after a long winter's rain, and he wanted her. "I promise."

He reached over and wrapped his hands around her hips, easily picking her up and setting her against the edge of the high mattress. He didn't join her on the dais. He leaned forward instead, kneeling down and pulling her long, smooth legs over his shoulders as he wedged himself between them.

"Remind me," he said then. "How did you want me to kneel? Like this?"

She muttered something that sounded like a prayer, or maybe it was his name.

"I'm not going to stop," he warned her, and felt her shudder against him. "I'm going to drown in you, and then I'm going to do it again. And again. Until I've had my fill."

She said something else, fervent and low and unintelligible. She was like a sensual banquet before him, her black hair a tangle around her head, her creamy skin flushed with desire, two scraps of erotic black lace framing that perfect body of hers, and all of it his.

"And I'm warning you, Zoe. That might take a while. I'm a greedy bastard."

She made a sound that was more like a sob. Hunter laughed.

He smoothed his hands up her silken thighs, drinking in each shiver, each tensing motion she made against him, around him. The black lace she wore was killing him, so sexy against her trim curves, her sweet skin. He could smell lavender again, and it made him even harder than he already was, bordering on desperate. She moved against him, against the bed, still making those noises that weren't quite words. Needy and mindless, and he was just getting started.

He wanted her screaming his name. He wanted her so badly it felt like a body blow. He didn't give a shit why she'd sought him out, only that she had.

"You're mine," he told her, fierce and sure.

He leaned forward and simply pressed his mouth against the center of her heat, black lace and woman, all Zoe and all his.

And then he feasted.

Chapter Seven

It was like dying.

Dying and then coming back to life, dressed all in fire, and Zoe couldn't catch her breath. There was only Hunter and that mouth of his, wild and demanding against the heart of her need. She found herself lolling back like a drunk, her arms over her face, panting desperately against the salt of her own skin.

He simply...took her. He kissed her, hard and intense through the lace of her boy shorts. He used his teeth, his tough jaw, that perfect mouth of his. She rocked against him, away from him, not sure what she wanted or what to do with the sensations that swept through her, each more overpowering than the last—

"Stop fighting me," he ordered her at one point, and her blood was rocketing so hard through her body, singing or screaming in her veins and she couldn't tell which, that she wasn't sure she heard him right.

"I don't know how," she gritted out. But she relaxed against him anyway.

Then he pressed his mouth against her again, harder, a gift and a discipline, and she splintered into a thousand pieces.

She was sobbing something incoherent, and he still didn't stop. She lost his mouth, but felt his hands at her hips again, and then a rush of cool air against all that heat, and it took her long moments to realize he'd stripped her panties from her without her noticing.

It occurred to her that even if the world was still spinning, even if she wasn't sure she knew her name or if she'd ever breath normally again, she should *do* something. Because somewhere beneath all of that shuddering, confounding pleasure that still stormed in her would be a price to pay. She knew that.

Too well.

Zoe struggled to move, to sit up, but found her limbs were far too heavy. As if they were his to command, not hers. She could only lie there, flushed and open and utterly destroyed, and watch him as he drew her legs back up over his shoulders, his blue gaze brilliant like diamonds, hot and hard on hers, and that look of sheer, male delight and satisfaction that made her chest hurt and her core ignite.

"I want…" It was too hard to speak, and that dangerous lassitude that had made her legs and arms feel so leaded was everywhere now, as if a great hand pressed her down into the bed from above, forcing her to lie there before him with such wanton abandon. "Let me…"

"I don't want to let you do anything," he told her. "I want to drown in you. I told you."

Then he slid his hands beneath her, propping her up before him like an offering, and she understood with a distant part of her brain—the only part that was still functioning— that the strange keening sound she heard was coming from her. But it didn't make sense, and he was looking at her, up over the length of her torso, his breath an intimate caress against the part of her that was the slickest and most sensitive, and she couldn't seem to stop shaking.

And there was too much calm certainty in that blue gaze of his, too much triumph in the crook of his mouth, and everything seemed to contract around them, inside her, until she thought they'd both gone electric.

Only then did he bend his head and lick into her.

And everything dimmed. Then exploded.

It was like being struck by lightning. Hit by it, torn wide open, then set afire again and again.

He teased her and taunted her. He used her own fire against her, growling into the molten core of her as he tasted her, so she could feel that wolf in him, feel it echo in every part of her. He pushed her and he adored her, worshipped her and taunted her, holding her right where he wanted her so there was no possibility of escape, as if he was prepared to force pleasure upon her if necessary.

And Zoe simply…surrendered to the storm.

To him. To Hunter.

As if she trusted him.

And when she flew apart this time, she could hear the dark sound of his laughter, the erotic triumph and the sensual delight, as if she was bathing in it.

Drowning, and she didn't care.

She was still fighting for breath when he moved, that terrible, wonderful mouth of his making its way over her hip, her belly. Lazy and knowing, building the fire in her all over again even as she still shook with the leftover flames of the previous blaze. He licked his way across her navel, climbing his way up her body as if he was committing every inch and every curve of her to memory, shifting her as he climbed, rolling them both toward the center of that massive bed.

He lifted her again, stripping her bra away and then worshipping her breasts, taking one hard nipple between his teeth, then sucking it hard into his mouth, shocking her with the intense shot of need that stormed through her all over again.

Impossible, she thought, and realized she'd moaned it aloud only when she felt laughter rumble through his big body.

"Not only possible," he said, insufferable and delicious at once, "but necessary."

"I'm very bored," she replied when she could form words, arching into him. "Will this take long?"

She didn't know why she felt compelled to tease him until she felt his teeth against her flesh, the little nip a punishment and a reward at once, and she smiled.

"You were right," he told her, his mouth against the tender side of her breast, his tough hands spread out over her back, keeping her arched up before him, his to feast on as he wished. "I use my body as a weapon. And you like it."

She felt his smile against her skin, then he turned his attention to her other breast, going back and forth between them with exquisite patience until she was writhing beneath him, as desperate and wild as if he'd only just begun. As if he hadn't thrown her over that cliff twice already.

"I need to taste you everywhere," he told her, that smile in his voice, in the press of his mouth to her flesh. "I can't get enough."

She felt the dangerous scrape of his teeth against her neck, the magic of his tongue. She explored his chest with shaking hands, the glorious strength in his cut shoulders, each taut ridge of his wonder of an abdomen she'd first seen rise before her from the water in that hot tub, sleek and warm. He smelled of something spicy and tasted of salt and man, and she couldn't get enough of him. When he crawled all the way up and settled himself between her legs, so hard and so big and so impossibly perfect, she almost toppled over that edge again, simply from the slick sweetness of the way they fit.

As if you were made for this, a little voice sang in her head. *For him.*

He propped himself above her, moving his hands to either side of her head and holding them there, and there was no sign of a smile on his beautiful face now, no trace of that laughter. There was only the stamp of need, a ferocity she felt deep within her. There was only that searing blue gaze, serious and intent.

Zoe's heart stuttered, then began to beat low and hard and long. She was cradling his tough, hard body with hers, and it turned her to liquid, molten and scalding.

"You want to be in control, don't you?" he asked, and everything about him was too dangerous, so dangerous it very nearly hurt. She could feel the press of him, pinning her to the bed, the hard thrust of him still in his trousers, but flush against her heat. Her need.

She'd had no idea it was possible to *need* anything this much. She wouldn't have thought she was capable of it. And yet it scalded her. It poured through her. It made her feel like someone else. Someone as strong as he was, and as dangerous.

As unbroken.

"Always," she managed to say, scraping together what remained of her bravado—but it came out sounding very nearly wistful, and she saw he felt that, too. In the way his blue eyes darkened. In the way he shifted against her, a roll of his hips that sent a delicious lightning bolt of a promise stealing through her, making her breath tight and erratic at once.

"I want to be inside you," he said. Like an invocation. "So deep you can't tell which one of us is which. So hard that when I come, you'll think it's you."

Heat coursed through her, pooling between her legs,

making her shift and roll, anything to feel that length of him hard against her softness, the next best thing—

"Zoe." It was a command. "Make it happen. Now."

She blinked, almost insane with wanting him. Understanding took a long, breathless beat, then another, as if her brain didn't want to work.

"You want me complicit."

"Absolutely no plausible deniability," he agreed, his gaze even hotter, making her restless beneath him.

"And if I don't do it?"

"I don't think that's going to happen." The wolf was in his eyes then, that hard curve of his mouth. Then in the way he moved his hips against hers again, making her breath hitch, sending more of that lightning crashing through her, flooding into all those dark places she'd locked away. "But if it does, you'll get to sleep empty and lonely and cold and alone. And in complete control. Is that what you want?"

"What if I can't decide?" She moved her hips with his, meeting him in that ancient dance, wrapping her legs around him and indulging herself in his steel length, pressed so hard against the part of her that needed it the most. Flames licked over her and she *needed*. She *wanted*. "What if this is enough for me?"

Hunter laughed, and then he dipped his head, and kissed her.

But it was better than a kiss. It stripped her bare. It was a carnal taking, a slick domination, and she thrilled to every slide of his tongue against hers, every hint of his teeth, the knowledge that he had the kind of willpower to hold them like this forever, slowly unraveling her. And that he would do it, if that was what it took.

He was using her body against her, and Zoe found she didn't care. She wanted him too much to worry about what that made her.

When he lifted his head, his eyes were so blue it hurt, and Zoe's hands were clumsy at the zipper of his unbuttoned trousers. She shoved and pushed and finally freed him, sighing when she wrapped her hands around the silken hardness of him.

But they were both too close to the edge. When he handed her a condom she noticed she was shaking again, and she could feel the slight tremors that moved in him, too, where he still held himself immobile above her.

She'd never wanted anything more. She sheathed him carefully, quickly, and then she guided him to her entrance.

"Say my name," he told her fiercely, the way he had before, with that curious intensity and that serious look on his face.

"I don't want to say your name," she threw at him, and she surged up before he could argue, impaling herself on the length of him.

It was slick, terrible, perfect.

Unreal.

"Why don't you say mine?" she managed to gasp, as if that might save her. As if anything could.

She understood she was doomed, and she didn't care anymore.

"Have it your way," he whispered, his mouth at her ear, and she was already shivering, already melting. Already his. "I'm going to make you scream it, Zoe. I'm going to make you beg. And then I'll do it all over again, until my name is the only thing you know."

"Promises, promises," she whispered, and laughed at the dark look on his face.

But then he began to move.

She was exquisite.

And she was his.

Hunter wanted to imprint that on her skin, tattoo it on the silken perfection of her flesh. He wanted to mark her, again, so there could be no doubt.

He settled for that simple, life-altering slide inside her, the clutch of her thighs, the sharp sting of her fingernails into his back. That complicated rhythm, that beautiful dance.

The animal in him wanted wildness—but he wanted to savor her, and so he did.

He set an easy, deliberate pace, stunned by the fire that roared inside him, drunk on each and every one of the noises she made, the motion of her lithe hips, the scent of lavender warm between their bodies, the taste of her and that sense of belonging, of *rightness,* that surged inside him, claiming him with every stroke.

Making him the man he should have been, as if this was

a baptism and he would never be the same when it was done. He believed it. He believed he could be anything for this woman. He wanted that as fiercely as he wanted her.

She tilted back her head, arched into him, and her eyes were dark with the same passion that he could feel in him. The same enormity. As if this wasn't sex, but a sacrament.

"Please," she gasped, and he smiled.

"I told you you'd beg."

"It's not polite to gloat," she said, and he didn't know how she did it, how she managed to sound so prim even now, when he was deep inside her and he held her on that quivering edge.

When the world felt new with every slick stroke, every glorious slide. Every shiver, every sigh.

It wasn't enough. It would never be enough.

"Say it," he told her. He lost himself in the taste of her breasts and toyed with those proud nipples, never changing his relentless rhythm, direct and deliberate, keeping her in that shaking frenzy beneath him but never quite tipping her over. "My name, Zoe."

And he felt her melt. Fire chased by lightning, soft and strong and *his,* and she cried it out at last. To the glass above, to the night around them, to the sky and to the world.

Again and again and again, until it sounded like a song. Like a vow.

His name. His possession. *His.*

"Hunter," she cried, "I'm going to kill you if you don't—"

"Didn't I promise to serve you? Have a little faith."

"Then do it, for God's sake!"

He laughed, reaching down between them and rubbing his fingers against the hard little heart of her, gathering her to him as she made a desperate noise that he felt in every part of him before she shattered all around him.

And only then, when she was in pieces again and he was drowning in her the way he wanted, the way he thought he might have to do for the rest of his life, until it killed him and he didn't think he'd mind if it did, did he let himself follow her over the edge.

Later, he woke in the stillness of the night in a sudden rush, but she was still there. She hadn't slipped out while he slept, while he wasn't paying attention. She hadn't disappeared. She hadn't walked away from him, never to be seen again.

His heart was pounding hard, as if he'd been running flat out for miles, and some part of him thought that he had been, one way or another, for the past ten years.

Not this time, he thought, with a solemnity that might have worried him in the light. But it was dark in his great cavern of a room, and the night wasn't nearly over, and he could pretend, for a moment or two, that he was the man he'd wanted to be while he was inside her.

Zoe was curled up against him as if they'd slept a thousand nights together exactly like this, and Hunter loved it. He loved the sweet scent of her hair and the fall of it through his fingers, the soft weight of her body against him in the dark. Her head pillowed on his arm and the way the delectable curve of her bottom fit so snugly against him in the middle of that vast bed, making it seem cozy.

She was smart and prickly, gorgeous and sexy, and she *fit* as if she'd been made to his precise specifications. She wasn't another groupie whose name he'd never learn. This hadn't been one more empty form of exercise. He'd wanted *her.* He still did. He felt it inside him, that ravenous burst of flame and something like wonder, and had the strangest feeling it wouldn't fade with the dawn like everything else.

He'd felt a pale imitation of this kind of rightness a long time ago, when he was young and callow, life was still golden and he hadn't the slightest idea what it was like to lose something irreplaceable. In the dark, he could admit to himself that this was different. This was better, if more complicated.

Because he still didn't know her plan. Why she'd hunted him down in that strip club and used Sarah to make him do what she wanted him to do. He still didn't know what she wanted from him.

Tonight, he didn't care.

She smelled of lavender and she'd tasted like sweet cream and hot, aroused woman, and he couldn't seem to react the way he ought to do. He couldn't seem to do anything but pull her closer, press a soft kiss to her temple and hold on to her as though he might not let go.

He moved behind her in the dark, tasting her all over again in the deep shadows, his hands exploring her, worshipping her as if it was the first time while he held her to him in that same position. He could trace the thrust of her breasts beneath her raised arm, kiss that sensitive spot behind her ear. He could smooth his way along her side, her thigh, her femininity warm and inviting beneath his hands. He could feel it when she transitioned from sleep to full alertness, and could feel, too, the delicious little shiver that moved in her then. When she thrust back against him with a small moan, pressing her bottom against him, making him that much harder.

When she whispered his name, he came inside her, making them both sigh. He rolled with her, holding her hand in his as he pressed her into the mattress. Like a dream. Hot like silk. Sweet.

And then he rode them both to that shattering end, slow and quiet and something like reverent. Like hope, he thought, losing himself in her.

Like a promise he intended to keep.

The morning light woke her, beaming in through all that glass with the frantic insistence of winter, and Zoe jolted up into sitting position. For a long moment, she had no idea where she was or why it was so *bright*.

And when it came back to her—when the long night before began to spool through her brain, one scalding-hot image after another, making her belly clench hard and deep all over again, tossing her right back into that fire—she was immediately furious with herself.

It was better than the darker things that lurked beneath that kick of temper—cleaner.

Waking up in his bed was not what was supposed to have happened. It was certainly not part of the plan she'd concocted on the fly last night, when she'd found herself kissing him and had understood she'd have to deal with this *thing* between them. With him.

Zoe should have left under cover of darkness, as she'd intended to do. After that first time. That she hadn't—the *reasons* she hadn't—made that dark well inside her yawn open even wider, even deeper. Even more treacherous than before.

She was such a fool.

Zoe had lost count of the number of times they'd come together in the darkness, and she didn't want to think about how often she'd been the one who'd reached for him. How she'd crawled over that athletic warrior's body of his entirely of her own volition, no masks and no games.

No hint of compulsion, only want. Need. Desire.

How she'd tasted every part of that mouthwatering torso of his, learning every inch of him, committing it to memory. How she'd taken his hard length in her mouth, licking it from stem to tip and back again, then teased the dark places below until he'd groaned out his surrender, his hands fisted in his sheets.

How she'd straddled him, taking him deep, so deep into her in a slick, exultant thrust that they'd both shuddered, and she'd had to brace herself against him for a moment to catch her breath—palms flat against the granite planes of his chest and the iron length of him driving her wild within.

She didn't want to think about the way his hands had gripped her hips as she'd started to rock herself on him, or the way she'd arched back to give him unfettered access to her breasts, her belly, and not because she'd wanted control—but because it felt good. So damned good it made her shiver again now, remembering it.

And she certainly didn't want to think about that shimmer of ecstasy that had wound in her, tighter and then tighter still, making her lose herself completely while he flipped her to her back and pounded them both straight into all of that stunning, glorious oblivion.

Hunter had been so fierce, and she'd matched it. So wildly possessive, and she'd returned it. Almost as if—

But she couldn't let herself go there. It didn't matter what had happened last night.

He'd had her. This was over. *That* was the plan.

Zoe scowled around at the ridiculous room, which seemed bigger and more severe with all that shattering winter sun pouring in, harsh and unavoidable. The wide bed stood at its center, a proud monument to a very long night she ought to regret. That the swirling darkness in her whispered she would regret, eventually.

At least Hunter was nowhere to be seen, for which she was grateful, she told herself.

That was what she felt, what that odd thing gnawing at

her was, making her pulse seem fluttery and too hard at once: *grateful*.

It was harder than it should have been to crawl out of that obnoxiously giant bed, over the dents in the soft pillows that whispered of Hunter. To look around for her underwear and her unfortunately slinky dress, which was the last thing she wanted to wear, maybe ever again, since all she could think about when she looked at it was Hunter. His hands. His mouth. His beautiful demands.

She'd felt strong. *Glorious*. As if she'd never been ruined. As if that was someone else.

It was then, as she stared down at the rumpled dress in her hands, that she understood what that great and dangerous pressure in her chest meant. That searing heat blinding her. That constriction in her throat that she didn't recognize, it had been so long.

She was about to break down and cry.

Zoe's hands curled into fists and she looked around wildly, ready to punch something, break something, scream—until she saw the doorway that led off to one side, almost hidden against the wall. It was through there, past acres of deep closets she shouldn't have had the slightest interest in exploring because she shouldn't have *cared,* that she found the sprawling bathroom. It held a bathtub that better resembled an Olympic-size swimming pool and a shower that could have housed multitudes, with at least three separate showerheads.

"The better to cater to a playboy lifestyle and all that it

entails," she muttered, her voice not even echoing in the exultantly luxurious space.

Groupies don't make it past the first floor, he'd said last night—and she hated how much she wanted to believe that now.

Zoe stood beneath the hot spray for a long time. Until her skin felt like hers again, as if it fit her once more, the way it was supposed to do. Until she stopped that helpless shaking, as though she was fighting off a fever. Until that hard, heavy weight shifted off her chest, and she was no longer afraid she might dissolve into tears.

Until the hot water washed away any evidence that some tears might have snuck out anyway, against her will.

She dried off, happy that she'd steamed up all the mirrors so she didn't have to look at her reflection, because she was afraid of what she might see. Too many truths in her eyes she didn't want to acknowledge. Too much she should have known better than to let herself feel.

"It was only sex," she told herself sternly as she climbed back into her clothes. She had to stop this. "Come on, Zoe. You've faced a whole lot worse than this."

And even though she knew that was true, it was so much harder than it should have been to start down those stairs once she'd twisted her hair back into a knot and pulled on her shoes. She made it to the first curve of the spiral stair, then stopped, shaking her head at herself. She swallowed, hard, and rubbed the heel of her hand against her chest, where that heavy weight had returned and hardened, become almost unbearable.

The trouble was, she liked him.

And as she stood there in last night's dress, her entire body still humming from the sleepless hours he'd spent branding every part of her with that wicked mouth of his, with every touch of his talented hands, Zoe felt as if she was cracked wide open. As if all of that sunlight pouring in from high above was ripping into her, through her, throwing open doors, shattering windows, knocking down walls.

She'd been hiding.

All this time, she'd been so proud of herself for moving on, for taking care of herself, for wresting a decent life out of the ashes of what had happened to her—but all she'd been doing was *hiding.* Holed up dreaming of revenge while the world turned on and on without her. Playing a game of survival across all these years.

But surviving wasn't the same thing as living. It wasn't even close.

Zoe looked down at herself, at the gray dress she wore, that was like all the other gray dresses she wore. Grays and blacks, dark browns and navy blues—she was wearing the colors of mourning. She'd been attending her own funeral for the past decade.

How had she failed to recognize that before now?

Any way she looked at it, standing here lit up and too bright after a night that shouldn't have happened with a man like Hunter who shouldn't have appealed to her at all, that meant Jason Treffen won. That he'd *been* winning since the day she'd escaped from his unsavory little operation and set out on her own. That on some level, this was all a game of pretend. Her fierceness, her insistence on control, *her whole life.*

Zoe pulled in a ragged breath. She shouldn't keep all the bright colors she allowed herself locked away in her apartment, like some kind of Miss Havisham in reverse. She shouldn't be afraid to be who she was, whoever that was. She wanted to feel the way Hunter made her feel—off-balance and alive. Wild and free and utterly unfettered. Even if that had all been run-of-the-mill on his part, his practiced playboy charm, it hadn't been on hers.

When Hunter kissed her, she felt whole.

That was winning. Reclaiming who she was, or who she might have been. Not hiding anymore. Not locking herself away, still fearful, she understood now, that Jason Treffen might reappear at any moment and tell the world what and who she really was.

As if that had ever been his call to make.

No wonder she'd been holding back from pushing her revenge plans into motion, even now when she was so close to the final act. No wonder it had taken so long. She'd still been afraid.

But she wasn't any longer. She felt free.

When she started down the stairs again, she was smiling, for what felt like the first time. Maybe ever.

She saw Hunter as she rounded the last bend, sprawled

out on that medicinally white couch of his, wearing nothing but a pair of exercise trousers low on his narrow hips. He looked sleepy and gorgeous, his dark blond hair rumpled and a hint of stubble on his jaw, making him look less pretty and more dangerous, which set off a little symphony of need inside her.

He made her feel insatiable. Greedy.

Beautiful and real.

Whole.

She moved toward him quietly, almost as if she was powerless to stop herself, and he didn't look up as she approached, too busy watching at the television screen in front of him with an intensity she didn't understand.

The volume was turned down so low she didn't hear *that voice* until she was right behind Hunter on the far side of the sofa.

That voice. Jason Treffen.

Hunter's television screen was so big it made Jason seem bigger than the wall. Bigger than life. Certainly big enough to destroy the tiny little lives he meddled in. Like Sarah's. Like hers. He lounged like the king of the world on some morning show couch, smiling genially, looking like the honorable and trustworthy man Zoe had once believed he was.

And Hunter sat there before his image, like the acolyte she'd somehow forgotten he'd been back then. Hell, maybe he still was.

That was why she'd chosen him.

The fact that she *liked* him was just her own twisted perversity at play.

Hunter turned to look at her. His eyes narrowed much too shrewdly as he sat up, as if he could read all manner of terrible things right there on her face. As though she wasn't maintaining that mask of hers any longer.

"Zoe?"

But she was looking at the screen, not at him.

"Zoe."

It was a command, but she was so far away then, so very far away, and it took a long time to pull her gaze away from the television and focus on the first man she'd let touch her in almost a decade. The first man she'd *wanted* in as long as she could remember. The first man she'd ever begged. The first man she'd liked like this in what she was fairly certain was forever.

Zoe didn't know why she was surprised that Jason Treffen should be hanging over this moment—literally. What was surprising was that she'd let herself forget that she knew exactly who Hunter was. That she always had.

"Tell me," Hunter said quietly. Intently. With some kind of reined-in ferocity that made the air feel heavy and unwieldy all around them. "How do you know Sarah?"

Maybe he knew, too. Maybe he'd always known, just as she had.

Maybe this was nothing more than another sick game.

But she was tired of everyone else winning. She was tired of hiding, no matter what had spurred her out into the light. She was tired of Jason fucking Treffen and the damage he did.

"I was there."

Zoe knew she was speaking only when she saw him react to her voice, jerking up and onto his feet as if she'd hauled off and hit him. But it was as though she'd vanished inside herself. Disappeared into that far-off safe space she hadn't had to access in a very long time. She could see how tense he was then and that terrible darkness on his face, but she actually smiled, because she'd gone completely and utterly numb, and it was better. Much better.

"I remember you, Hunter."

"You're going to have to be more specific."

There was a dark torment in his gaze, in the odd tautness in his body, in the way he started to reach for her, then stopped.

Of course he stopped. She suspected he knew exactly what she was going to say. And who wanted to touch someone like that? She couldn't blame him.

It was lucky she'd disappeared inside herself, because even that didn't hurt.

"Sarah and I met at orientation at Treffen, Smith, and Howell when we still thought we were going to be legal assistants," Zoe said in that remote and chilly way, as if she wasn't really talking about herself. And in so many ways, she wasn't. That Zoe had died a long time ago. "She wanted to be a judge someday. I wanted to say clever things in court. We ate lunch together every day, though as time passed, we talked less. That last week we just sat there, because what was there to say?" To his credit, he didn't look away. But then, maybe he already knew all of this. "She wasn't the only one who killed herself, you know. She just did it spectacularly."

He said something and it took her a moment to realize it was her name.

"She always said you were her boyfriend," Zoe said, because she didn't care what he said or even how he said it. As if it was painful. "It didn't occur to me until later that you were already very wealthy at twenty-three. Were you really her boyfriend? Or did you pay more so she'd act like it?"

Hunter went pale, and it was like a kick to the belly that some part of her responded to that, *hurt* for him.

"I did not pay Sarah to do anything," he said, in a stranger's voice. As if he wanted to be pissed she'd suggested it, but it hurt too much.

"Did he blackmail you?" she asked coolly, telling herself none of the rest of it mattered. And it didn't. *He* didn't. He was useful, nothing more. "Because that's what he does. It's not enough to run escorts out of a fancy law firm. Not for a saint like Jason Treffen."

"I didn't pay Sarah." Still that dark, awful tone in his voice. "I didn't pay anyone."

"I assumed you got fired from your football team because you stopped paying him off." Zoe held his gaze, and it wasn't bravado that moved in her then. It was much heavier than that. Much more poisonous. "But that only works if you were one of his johns. If you still are."

"No." His voice was low and altered, as if he was forcing it out through steel wool and it was scraping deep marks into him along the way. "That was all me. I was expelled from the NFL purely because I'm an asshole."

Jason Treffen hung on the wall on the television screen behind him, framing Hunter the way he'd framed Zoe's life, and she wished she could summon up the anger that usually fed her—the deep, abiding fury that had fueled her all these years. Jason laughed, Jason flirted with the two morning show hosts, Jason played his fucking part the way he always did, and she wished she had access to the rage that had kept her warm and safe and alive this past decade.

But she felt that weight on her chest, pressing behind her eyes, and she felt nothing but sad. So terribly sad she thought it might warp her. Change her. Disfigure her down into her bones, so deep and so permanent that she'd never walk the same way again.

There was always a price. For everything. She knew that better than anyone.

Zoe supposed she shouldn't be so surprised that after all this time, after all the ways she'd paid and paid, it could still hurt like this.

And yet there it was, tearing her up as if she hadn't been quite as ruined as she'd thought. As if there was always something new that could be leveled. Razed. Turned to dust.

"Aren't we a pretty pair," she said, all of that darkness in her voice, all these years of despair and denial and revenge fantasies to ease the terrible cost of it all.

Everything she'd done. Everything she'd lost. All the girls Jason had ruined. All the ways she was ruined herself. *All of it.* Because that was all she had left.

Maybe Jason had been right a long time ago, and what he'd made her was all she'd ever be. Maybe she should have surrendered to that a long time ago, the way so many of the others had. The way Sarah had.

Maybe she should have given up. It would have been easier.

She smiled at Hunter, and told herself this was funny. "You're not a john, but at least you get to be an asshole. I'm afraid I'm just another whore."

Chapter Eight

He'd known.

On some level, Hunter was aware, he'd suspected this. Why else would she have thrown Sarah's name in his face that first morning?

He'd known, but he hadn't wanted to know. The story of his fucking life, and yet this wasn't the time to dive back into the comfortable swamp of his own self-pity. Not when she'd gone too cold, too frigid. And it wasn't that clever, deliberate coolness he'd found he couldn't get enough of, that he only wanted to bask in. It was as though the Zoe he'd known had disappeared beneath a long winter's deposit of ice, and he could hardly bear it.

He hated it. He wouldn't allow it. He crossed his arms over his chest to keep from reaching out to her, and he drew on all his years of tense football games and tough plays to calm himself down. To focus. This wasn't about him, it was about Zoe. His beautiful, brave, tough Zoe, who he refused to let disappear into that darkness he could see had its hooks in her. Deep.

"This is why you wanted me," he said, straining with the effort to keep from shouting. To keep all that fury that rolled inside him banked and controlled, because he didn't want to aim it at her. "My connection to Sarah." He jerked his head at the television screen. "To that piece of shit."

"You're the key to my revenge," she agreed. But her voice was frozen. Too sharp and mocking. It was like a slap.

He didn't want to slap back, he wanted to soothe her, hold her, *help* her—but he knew she'd never let that happen. She'd never let him close to her again without a fight.

Hunter could always fight. He was good at it.

"Some revenge," he said. "So enthusiastically sleeping with a man you think prefers the company of call girls. How does that hurt Jason, exactly?"

"That was purely to manipulate you." A quirk of her dark brows. "Especially the enthusiasm."

He laughed, though he couldn't quite pull it off. "I appreciate you suffering through it. Very thoughtful. But you probably should have come up with a better morning-after act."

There was a flicker of something in her too-dark eyes then, and he thought he might have broken through, but then she only smiled that same empty smile.

"I don't think I have to manipulate this situation any further," she said calmly. Too calmly, as if he hadn't been there in that bed. As if he didn't know there hadn't been a shred of calculation in her all night long. "You're either going to help me because Jason Treffen is responsible for your girlfriend's death, or because you know I'm aware that you're one of his very special clients and you wouldn't want that getting out. It doesn't matter which."

"Of course it matters." That came out harsher than it should have, revealing him too starkly, and her head jerked back as if he'd hit her. *Damn it.* "I told you I was never his client. Not like that." He studied her for a taut breath, then another. "Are you fighting all the ghosts in the room or are you fighting me? I can't tell."

"I can't really see the difference."

"Fight me, Zoe. You can actually hit me. Because I'm standing right here."

She moved then, and he thought it was a small sort of victory, even when all she did was head to the far end of the sectional and sit down, lounging back as if she'd never been more at her ease. Never more calm.

Meanwhile, he thought his chest might crack wide open. He thought this might actually kill him. Especially when she leveled that unfriendly look at him, as though after all of this, he was the enemy.

"I'm not fighting," she said, in a tone that suggested he was a raving lunatic.

Hunter rubbed his hands over his face, then sat down, too, not far from her but certainly not as close as he would have liked. There was too much boiling inside him, too big and too dangerous, and all of it so painful and unbalanced and extreme he didn't know what to do with any of it.

"Of course you're not," he muttered, and instead of indulging his usual fight-or-fuck response to adversity the way he'd have preferred, he just looked at her. "Why don't you tell me this plan of yours? I think it's time for the great unveiling, don't you?"

She was quiet for a moment, and Hunter was too aware of the way his heart pounded so damned hard, how his breath felt caught in his chest. Loud. Constrained. Zoe shifted slightly where she sat, and he wanted it to be nerves. He wanted her to feel some of what he did.

"The plan is that you expose Jason Treffen. Show the world who he really is." She gave him that small, sharp smile again, still lacking the bite and sparkle of the Zoe he knew. "Right before his big interview that will cement him in the public imagination as a saint forevermore."

"Why would anyone listen to me?" He was proud of his calm, reasonable tone. "I don't know if you've been paying attention, but I'm not exactly considered the poster boy for truth and justice these days."

"That's why you're perfect." She seemed to relax slightly as she ticked off his selling points on her fingers, one after the next. "Your reputation is already shot, so it's not as if Jason can threaten you with the loss of it. You're hated, in fact, so what will it matter if people hate you more? But you also have intimate knowledge of the man going back more than a decade, which means that if you speak out long enough and loud enough—and into the right ears, which is where I come in—you'll eventually be heard." She smiled again. "And meanwhile, the fact that you've spent all this time quietly doing good works in the wake of your expulsion from the NFL without attempting to benefit personally from any of it will, of course, play heavily in your favor."

"And here I was beginning to think you were making it up as you went along."

She shrugged. "I told you I knew what I was doing."

But he couldn't help thinking about how she'd have said that last part if she wasn't as switched off and distant as she was now, and it thudded inside him, the loss of her sharp, knowing smirk. Of that amused glint in her cool gray gaze.

He wanted her back.

"I was hoping you were going to these lengths because you had designs on my fine body. It happens. Sometimes, as you saw, it even happens at the gym. Or in libraries."

"Maybe you didn't hear me before," she said, much too softly, her gaze dark and tormented on his. "I wasn't being metaphoric. I was an escort. I sold myself. To men. For money." Each sentence was a short, harsh bullet. "Why would you keep flirting with me now? This is usually where I get paid. That's what *whore* means."

And Hunter recognized what he saw in her, then. What she was doing.

That almost-warm, near-laughter in her voice, encouraging him to join in the horrible joke. That sharp, pointed boldness, throwing the worst thing she could think of out on the table like that. And all of that terrible anguish beneath.

Oh, yes. He knew this routine. So well he could taste it like bile in his own throat.

He knew terrible guilt when he saw it. He knew self-loathing and that deep, debilitating shame. He knew this game. He'd been playing it for years, and with far less reason.

But he also knew Zoe.

"How do you want to be paid?" he asked lazily, and she jerked against the sofa, her breath leaving her in an audible rush. "Cash? Credit card? An exchange of gifts and services?"

She looked as if he'd hit her again, and harder this time. "Very funny."

"Let's be clear, Zoe. I don't think anything that's happened since you came downstairs this morning is funny. Not in the least. I asked you a question."

"About payment." She'd gone still. Pale.

He thought that was probably progress, though it felt like broken glass inside him, shattering over and over again.

"Sure." He held her gaze, hard. Until she let out a long, shaky breath, temper and agony, and he felt it like nails across his chest. "Name your price."

"Stop." Small, but certain.

"You seem to want to throw what happened to you in my face, so let's do this. Let's make it as awful as possible. Name a price. You know I can pay it. I'm richer than God."

"Of course you're making this about you. That's what men like you—"

"There are no men like me," he bit off, all the violence he was holding in check in his voice then. "Not for you. Not now. *Name your price.*"

"Go to hell!" she threw at him.

She surged to her feet in a blind explosion, but he'd expected that. Wanted it. He met her, feeling a kind of deep satisfaction when she swung at him. He felt her fists land on him, harder than he'd anticipated, and he let her do it. He didn't even raise his own arms in defense.

"Hit me harder," he told her gruffly, watching that dark light in her eyes, that grim cast over her face. "Make it hurt, Zoe, or what's the point?"

She swayed on her feet, her breath coming in harsh pants, but the gray eyes that met his were a wild winter storm. The dead thing behind them was gone, and though he knew that was good, he also knew it must hurt. And still she held her fists in front of her like weapons, as if she had no idea how small they were. Or as if it didn't matter, because she'd fight anyway.

His Zoe. Completely incapable of surrender.

"Hurt me," he said again, more intently. "Don't you know how this works? Shit always rolls downhill. So consider this an incline."

She was still breathing too hard. She looked forlorn and terrified and fierce all at once, and he knew that if he tried to touch her she'd come straight out of her skin. He concentrated on the faint sting from the blows she'd landed on his chest, each one proof she wasn't as lost as she looked.

She hadn't disappeared beneath that ice. She was still right here, no matter how much it hurt her. Or him.

"I don't want to hurt you," she gritted out after a long moment, as if the words were torn from her throat.

He waited until her gaze moved to meet his again. Held it. "Then don't."

"It's not that simple."

"Yes," he said. Implacable. Sure. When he was neither of those things in anything but this. "It is."

Zoe jerked her head away, turning it to the side as if that would hide the way her face crumpled in on itself, and he had to stand there and watch that. Stand and do nothing but *wait* while she pressed one of those tight fists to her lips, as though she could beat back her own tears if she had to. If it came to that.

"Let's hurt the person who deserves it," Hunter said quietly, and though she didn't look back at him then, though he saw the hint of moisture at the corners of her eyes and the fist at her mouth tightened until her knuckles went white, Zoe nodded. It was jerky and stiff, and it seared straight through him as if it was his own pain, but it was a nod. "As it happens, I have a few ideas of my own."

He called Austin from the car as he drove toward Edgarton that afternoon, the way he'd done every afternoon since Zoe had taken him there. First because she'd ordered him to do it and he'd decided to take that ride. And then only partly because of that, though that was one more thing he wasn't ready to think about.

"Who is this?" Austin asked in lieu of a greeting. "I don't recognize this number. I'm pretty sure the previous owner accused me of being a stalker."

"We need to meet," Hunter said, ignoring the dig.

"I definitely don't recognize this voice. You know you can't keep playing the head-in-sand routine if you call meetings, right? People might get the wrong impression and think you care about something."

"Tomorrow night. I don't care where. Bring Alex."

"Alex is actually a grown man, Hunter, with his own very busy schedule, which you would know if you ever took his calls. I don't keep him in my back pocket."

"There's someone I want you both to meet," Hunter said impatiently, and he didn't know if it was his tone of voice that did it or the fact that there could really be only one reason he'd want to make introductions to the two of them, but Austin was quiet for a moment.

"Who?"

Zoe had said she was fine with this, that she wanted to do it because it dovetailed so nicely with her own plans, but Hunter still wanted to protect her if she changed her mind. Because this might be the only way she'd ever let him protect her, he thought darkly, and the truth was she was far more likely to simply punch him again.

He let it sit there a moment, the realization that he'd take either one.

"You'll find out tomorrow," he said gruffly to Austin. "Unless you want to lecture me more about my telephone habits? Compare me to an ostrich again? I'm sure you can insult me much better than this, Austin. It's like you're not even trying."

"Hunter."

He waited, and it was as if history and memory compressed, somehow. As if it snapped tight in both of them at that same moment, reminding him of a thousand other phone conversations, as many long, late nights, all those hours upon hours they'd spent in each other's company learning their own private language, making themselves their own form of family.

Reminding him again how much they'd lost.

"Listen," he began, inadequately, because he was pretty sure this was all his fault. He was the one who'd left. The one who'd never looked back. The one who'd been so determined to pretend nothing was happening, then or now.

But Austin was talking again. Heading him off as if he already knew where this was going.

"It better not be a fucking florist," he said, and Hunter couldn't help but grin. "I'm not kidding."

The Edgarton High football field lay under two feet of fresh snow and likely would for weeks, which meant these practices took place indoors in the old, drafty gym.

Hunter hated the gym.

The scratched-up floors bent and squeaked beneath the

pummeling of so many adolescent shoes, the smell of damp surrounded them like a humid choke hold, and the small, high windows were much too far from the ground to let in what little winter light was available.

The whole depressing place was a fire hazard.

Didn't they fire your ass? Aaron, the punk wannabe quarterback, had demanded that first day. The kid had been puffed up and scowling as if he thought he was a much bigger man. But that hadn't concealed the dazed longing in his dark eyes, letting Hunter know how badly he'd wanted to be convinced Hunter was the real deal. That something— *anything*—was. *Why should I listen to anything you say?*

Because I'm a goddamned legend, Hunter had retorted. *And you suck.*

And yet, defying all reason and his own uncertain temper, his small, sad group of kids not only kept coming to his increasingly difficult weight sessions and his killer drills—all better suited to teams that were already at the championship level than one with their decided lack of skills, because Hunter thought they might as well start hard—but they seemed to bring more new players with them each time they came. Until it looked less like an afterthought in that weight room, that sad old gym, and more like an actual team.

Today the sight of them made him harsher. More demanding. Because he refused to fail anyone else.

He refused.

"You, uh, doing okay?" Jack, the actual football coach, not that anyone had been observing that title in weeks, dared to ask him. Hunter had the team running speed drills. Again and again and again, up and down the length of the old gym floor, pretending he couldn't hear the mutinous grumbling as they went.

"They have to be able to do this perfectly when they're exhausted," Hunter said shortly. "It's about mental toughness."

"Yeah," Jack said, in one of those too-agreeable voices that meant he didn't want to argue, not that he actually agreed. "Sure. But, um. Are *you...?*"

"I'm fine," Hunter bit out, short and rough.

Jack flinched, but Hunter couldn't seem to modify his tone. Not when he was angrier than he'd ever been, and he couldn't do a single thing about it. He couldn't fix Zoe. He couldn't save her. He couldn't change a single thing that had happened to her, just as he hadn't been able to save anyone else. Sarah. Even himself.

He couldn't even touch her the way he wanted, because that wasn't what she needed. She'd said he'd made it about him and he, by God, refused to let that happen. He'd take Jason Treffen apart with his own hands if that was what it took—

He realized he was scowling, and that Jack was staring at him.

"Why?" he asked. It came out in a growl. "Do I not seem fine?"

Jack raised his hands in surrender and didn't ask again.

"You can decide what kind of losers you want to be," he

told the pack of kids later that same bitterly cold evening. They were panting on the floor at his feet, stretched out across the scratched gym floors with the drafty walls letting too much winter in. Looking as if they thought they might die—or had already died. Which meant that he must have been doing something right. "The kind who gives the better team a fight or the kind who wastes everyone's time. Entirely up to you, gentlemen."

There was a long, angry, tired sort of silence. He almost smiled.

"You get to decide who you are," he continued, arms over his chest, scowl firm on his face. "You either get up and keep playing when it hurts, or you hobble off the field and you don't come back. Very few choices in life are this simple. Relish this one."

"Says the guy who got booted a month before the Super Bowl," someone muttered.

"And is fighting, like, twenty lawsuits," someone else replied, to a smattering of laughter.

"I wish I saw some of that smart-assed spirit in these drills," Hunter snapped, and the laughter died off. "Understand this right now—you're the only people in the entire world who give a shit what happens to you. You might not like my choices, but for better or worse, they were all mine. Now make yours. Get up. We're running another drill."

It was hard not to smile at the moaning then, and he wasn't sure he succeeded.

"If you can't handle it, leave now," he barked. "Your choice."

"What do you know about choices?" Aaron, who was apparently not smart enough to act appropriately cowed by all of Hunter's bluster, demanded as he got to his feet. "Not like this is anything more than a vacation for you. We'll still be here long after you get bored and go back to your real life."

"Are you here to make friends?" Hunter growled, staring the kid straight in the eyes. "Sing happy songs and braid each other's hair? Is that why you keep coming here, Aaron? Or do you want to suck slightly less at football?"

And he saw it then: that hint of steel on the kid's face. The way he stood straighter, though he must have wanted to eat and sleep more than he wanted his next breath. As if he'd decided, then and there, that he wanted *this* more. Even if it was only to show Hunter that he could.

That was how it began, Hunter knew. He remembered it, as if it was from a different life. That drive to be something else. To be better.

"Don't worry, dude," Aaron said with a sneer, something flashing in his dark eyes that made Hunter feel something very much like proud. "I wasn't picking out my prom dress just yet. You can calm down."

"While you can give me fifty push-ups," Hunter retorted. "And if you don't learn how to speak respectfully, you'll be doing them all night. *Dude*."

And it wasn't until he had the team running drills, Jack starting to shout out commands from the sidelines as if he was feeling like a coach himself, Aaron counting out his push-ups in a markedly more polite tone, that Hunter allowed himself that smile.

This was a lot harder than she'd anticipated.

Zoe ducked out of the cold wind in a recessed doorway halfway down the block from the bar where she was supposed to meet Hunter, her heart clapping so hard against her ribs she thought it might leave bruises.

It was one thing that Hunter knew about her past. A horrible, deeply upsetting thing that she'd spent a whole day trying and failing to come to terms with. But why had she agreed to walk into a public place and tell two more people the secret she'd hidden away all these years?

Especially when one of them was a Treffen.

For a terrifying moment, she couldn't breathe.

She didn't know how long she stood there, fighting off the panic. Would she simply fall apart where she stood? Right there on the street? Was it wrong that some part of her wanted that, so at least she wouldn't have to talk about this again? But slowly, she pulled air into her lungs. One long breath, then another. Eventually, she stood straight. Calm. And when all that noise in her head had quieted, she made herself walk out into the flow of foot traffic again, then the rest of the way down the block, as if she was fine.

Because she *was* fine. She was.

She had to be fine, one way or another.

Because she could hardly expect to take down the monster who still lurked in every single one of her nightmares if she couldn't have a simple conversation with two men who, Hunter had assured her, hated Jason Treffen as much as she did.

Hunter. His name in her head, her heart, like a drumbeat. Images of him in that bed, on top of her, inside her. His face, tormented and drawn, when he'd told her to *hit him harder*—

She couldn't bear that he knew. She couldn't stand it. It made her feel wobbly inside, as if she might dissolve at any moment. But she had no choice but to pretend she was made of stone instead.

She never had any choice.

The bar in question was a private club in a boutique hotel. There were two actual velvet ropes and a stone-faced sentry at the final door to navigate before Zoe was admitted to the enclosed rooftop space. It offered views of the quiet Lower East Side street below with the immensity of Manhattan looming everywhere above them, filled with a noticeably elegant and star-studded crowd there, no doubt, to bask in its exclusivity.

It was pretty. She could breathe.

She was fine.

"Zoe."

She stiffened, more ice than stone, but it was Hunter, pushing himself away from the wall near the entrance to meet her. And then she hated herself, because she'd let him see her reaction. It was as if she didn't fit in her own skin anymore. It made her feel things she'd gone to great lengths to keep from feeling for all these years. Vulnerable. Small.

She watched his too-clever eyes narrow, knowing he saw too much. As usual, damn him.

And then she hated him, too, because he didn't reach over and touch her. Oh, no. No fingers at her cheek, no touch against the hair she'd let fall around her shoulders tonight. Hunter thrust his hands into the pockets of his trousers and he stood too close, so close she could almost feel that drugging heat of his—but he didn't touch her the way she knew he would have before.

Before she'd told him the truth about what she was. Before he'd discovered that she wasn't that incandescent creature she'd seen reflected in his gaze when he'd moved inside her.

Before.

It was only to be expected, but that didn't make it any easier. And she hated that it hurt. So much more than it should have.

"Let's do this," she blurted out, with perhaps a touch too much aggression. He blinked.

"You don't have to do anything." His voice was so calm. A hint of his drawl, no sign of temper or pain or heat. "You don't have to meet them. You can turn around right now and leave. I'll still do whatever you want me to do to help bring him down. You don't have to involve anyone else if you don't want to."

"I want to." Her lips felt numb, but that didn't matter. So did her heart. She'd do this anyway. "Let's go."

But Hunter didn't move. He frowned down at her, his gaze moving over her face, and she felt nothing but a howling within. Because he'd wanted to touch her so badly he shook with it, before. And now he knew how filthy she was, how polluted, he kept his hands to himself. She hadn't imagined he'd be any different from the whole rest of the world, so there was no reason that should feel like a punch in the stomach. Like betrayal.

No reason at all.

She unzipped the coat she wore with more force than skill, then unwound her scarf from around her neck, scowling at him as she did it.

"Hunter. I said I want to do this, which means sometime tonight, please."

"What are you wearing?"

Zoe knew what he meant, but there was temper and heartache and panic pounding at her temples, in her veins, in every breath she took, and she wanted to hit him again. Harder this time. With something very heavy, like one of the nearby tables.

"I believe we call them *clothes*." She eyed him, hoping she looked as unfriendly as she felt. As she wished she felt. "But you can call them whatever you want. I don't really care."

He blinked again, and she thought he tensed, but when he spoke again his voice was still perfectly smooth. If a shade darker.

"I've never seen you in jeans before." He said it as if it hurt his jaw. "Or red."

"It's been a big week. Why not reflect it in my wardrobe?"

His gaze moved over her, and she hated the fact her body responded, shivering into the heat of it, letting that damned *need* bloom wherever that blue gaze touched.

"I like it," he said.

"That was, of course, my singular goal."

His mouth crooked then, as if he knew. As if he'd been there tonight when she decided it was time to come out of her Ice Queen cave of sleek mourning clothes. As if he knew perfectly well that she'd been unable to get that hot gleam in his blue gaze out of her head when she'd pulled on the dark black skinny-legged jeans that hugged her legs and the red top that wrapped around her torso, leaving a deep V open in front. As if he knew exactly what she'd been thinking when she slid on the killer heels in a leopard print that demanded attention and did wicked things to her walk, especially on wintry sidewalks.

As if she was completely and utterly transparent, after all these years of hiding herself away.

And that same fire licked at her, reminding her. The air between them pulled taut. She saw that awareness in his gaze, that same bright blaze.

But he still didn't make a single move to touch her, and that burned through her like poison, drowning out everything else, sitting heavy on her chest like the tears she refused to cry. Not here. Not in front of him. Not when it already hurt this much.

She wanted to scream, to swing out at him, to burst—

"Come on," he said quietly, using his chin to point the way, as if even the smallest touch would be corrosive. As if she was *infectious*. It was her worst nightmare come true, and this man had been *inside* her. She felt nauseated, and then furious at herself for expecting anything different. "They're over here."

Zoe would have said her heart had been ripped out such a long time ago that it couldn't break any further. That it couldn't possibly crack the way it did then, shattering into all those jagged pieces that cut at her every time she breathed in.

But she walked where he pointed her anyway, because it was better than falling apart. She'd have to save that for later, when this was over. When Hunter couldn't see her do it. When she could make sure he'd never, ever know. That no one would.

Alex Diaz and Austin Treffen waited at a private table far in the corner, and both stood when she appeared, both as good-looking and obviously powerful as she'd expected. Zoe told herself they were like any other clients. Rich, accomplished and probably evil. It was always best to assume that from the start. Fewer surprises, she'd always found.

She supposed it said something about her that the thought soothed her.

"I don't need an introduction," she said, pulling her professional persona around her like a cloak and even forcing a smile, surprised when it came easily. As if nothing had changed, even if it felt as though everything had. "I know who you are." She shook hands the way she always did, brisk and confident, as if she felt either. "Alex. Austin. I'm Zoe Brook."

"The PR queen of New York," Alex said, smiling in that intent way she assumed reporters always did, and she wasn't at all surprised he was as successful as he was. "Of course. It's nice to meet you in person, though your reputation precedes you."

"Better than a florist, I guess," Austin said. Bizarrely. But he was staring at Hunter. "Are *you* worried about your reputation, Hunter? Because I think that's a lost cause."

"Zoe has a particular affinity for Saint Jude, as a matter of fact," Hunter said, and there was clearly something wrong with her that the reference warmed her. He thought she was toxic and she was getting soft over a throwaway line about a martyr. She wasn't sure who she hated more just then, herself or him.

Him, she decided, when he maneuvered her so he was sitting in the booth with his buddies and she was on the outer edge. Was he afraid she'd spill her filth all over his friends? Get them as dirty as she was—as dirty as she'd made him?

Far inside her, something keened. A horrible, grieving sound, made of loss and regret, but she ignored it. There was no point to it. There was no fixing anything. There was only revenge, and no matter what she felt about Hunter beneath all of the shattered pieces and the poison and all the ways she'd been tainted by what she'd done, she believed what he'd said. That revenge would work better with Alex and Austin involved.

Assuming they were who he said they were.

"What are we doing here?" Austin asked. He looked at Zoe and smiled slightly. "If you'll excuse my impatience."

She smiled back, and was pleased on some level when Hunter tensed, as if he knew what was coming.

"I hate wasting time," she said. "It's a pet peeve of mine."

"Zoe."

That was Hunter, of course. But she'd clicked back into her professional mode, and it was a relief. She was bullet-proof when she was this version of herself. Fully armor-plated. She could even relax against the booth as if this was a garden party and she was here to discuss nothing more dramatic than canapés. A friendly game of croquet. What-ever the rich and bored drawled about while wreathed in all their privilege.

"Your father is a pimp," she told Austin coolly, and watched his eyes go blank with some mix of resignation and temper she didn't know him well enough to decipher. She glanced over at Alex, who had gone very still himself. "And I remember both of you from the halcyon days of my time as a legal assistant at Treffen, Smith, and Howell back when your friend Sarah Michaels worked there, which, yes, means exactly what you think it does."

She heard Hunter sigh from beside her, where he sat close

but still not touching her. Zoe understood that he never would again, and she refused to mourn that. She'd wanted to use sex only to end the tension between them and make him more malleable. She should have been thrilled it had been a success.

A great big fucking *success,* and what she really hated him for, she thought then, was that he'd made her feel whole and new only to turn around and make it clear that she'd never be anything but broken. It was the truth, but that didn't make it any easier to bear.

She leaned forward and propped her elbows on the table, as if this was a casual chat among friends.

"Hunter assures me that he was never one of the many johns Jason pandered to and then blackmailed," Zoe said, almost sweetly. She smiled, and she watched both Alex and Austin closely. "What about you two?"

Chapter Nine

As introductions went, it was explosive, Hunter thought, as she'd no doubt intended.

Zoe sat there so calmly beside him, looking perfectly at ease, as if she discussed prostitution and blackmail and human perversity every night of the week. As if he hadn't seen the scars of her past alive and bright on her face in his own living room only yesterday. As if it had all happened to someone else.

"My mother is finally divorcing my father," Austin said, once Zoe looked more convinced than not that he and Alex weren't monsters. "I'm happy to say I helped her reach that decision and that I'm representing her. If I had my way I'd leave him bloody and beaten on the courtroom floor, but I'll settle for taking as much of his money as possible."

"Must we choose?" Zoe asked coolly.

Hunter had never admired anybody more.

"You need to tell this story, Zoe," Alex told her then, his voice intense. He leaned forward. "The call girls. The blackmail of all those clients. The world needs to know the truth about him."

"I agree," Zoe said, collected and cool, as always. "But I can't do that."

"You must know that first-person, witness, *victim* testi-mony—"

"I was his victim for too long," she said so smoothly it took a moment to feel the edge in it, the blade. "I won't do it again."

It was quiet for a moment, a hush over their table while the rest of the club glittered and murmured all around them. Austin's expression was even darker than usual, while Alex only studied Zoe, as if looking for a way past that smooth wall of hers. *Good luck with that, buddy,* Hunter thought, but shifted closer to her, in case he tried.

"I understand where you're coming from," Alex began, as if he was choosing each word carefully.

"Do you think so?"

That time her voice was so light, so very nearly buoyant, that it took them all a minute to understand that it was a gut punch. Then to feel it.

"I wish I could impress upon you—" Alex began again.

"Enough." Hunter didn't know he meant to speak until he heard his own voice. It was an implacable command, barked out as if he was still the quarterback who expected his orders to be followed immediately.

Alex looked at him, then back at Zoe. He didn't look happy, but he nodded.

"Why don't we talk strategy?" Zoe asked, sounding utterly unruffled, but Hunter knew her now. He *saw* her.

Her pulse betrayed her in that hollow at her neck, the hand she held in her lap—beneath the table where only he could see it—was balled into a tight fist, and the leg she'd crossed over the other was too taut, too stiff.

And Hunter despaired of himself, because even now, even here, he wanted her.

If he was a better man, he wouldn't, surely. Not now. He would simply protect her the way she should have been protected from the start. If he could, he would have kept her safe from vermin like Jason Treffen in the first place. He would have saved her. Instead, he was part of the problem. He was disgusted with himself.

Zoe was outlining the same plan she'd shared with him, in her usual concise way. Hunter had no doubt that it would work, eventually. He believed she was as good as she said she was. But he didn't want the slow build, the right word placed delicately in the right ear. He wanted swift, decisive action.

He wanted Jason cut down and cut off. Now.

"It's not enough," he said when she was done. Zoe took a breath before she looked at him directly, and her gaze was too dark on his, as if he'd hurt her. But he couldn't seem to help that, and what he wanted to do would help more, in the end. "It turns into an extended battle for public opinion, possibly allowing him to win."

"He won't," Zoe said, a frosty edge to her voice.

"He might. Why allow the possibility?"

"Because in addition to all your other well-documented skills, you're now an expert on PR?" she asked in that sharp tone that he found he still loved, even when it lacerated him. "Oh, no. Wait. That's me."

"I keep telling you, it takes a tremendous amount of skill to climb to the many heights I have and fall straight down from each and every one of them."

"Keep calling it a skill if that makes you feel better."

"You don't know Jason as well as we do," he said, trying to pull the others back into the conversation, aware that they were watching the interchange between him and Zoe a little too closely for his liking.

"And you don't know him the way I do," she said, fierce and hollow at once.

Hunter inclined his head, conceding the point.

"But wrecking his reputation isn't enough. He's already lost his family, thanks to Austin. Alex is plotting his downfall in the media. There's something better you and I can do. That *only* we can do."

She shifted so she could really look at him then, and Hunter forgot where they were. Who was sitting with them, watching all of this. But he didn't care. Not when there was a storm in those dark gray eyes of hers, seeing things in him he'd never been able to hide. Not from her.

"This from the man I found in a strip club," she said softly. Harshly. A kill shot, he understood. "Who wanted to do absolutely nothing but marinate in his own self-pity for the rest of his life."

Austin laughed. Alex winced. And Hunter was obviously as slow as he sometimes acted, because it was only then he realized that she was very, very angry with him.

Hunter made himself breathe in slow, then let it out slower. As if he was back on the football field. He blocked everything else out. The blow she'd just delivered with such deliberate precision. That awful, betrayed look in her eyes. The noise from the bar around them, the clinking of expensive glasses and the muffled sounds of Manhattan high life on all sides. He shunted it all aside and focused solely on the goal: Jason Treffen.

"Do you want to win this argument or do you want your revenge?" he asked her, straight and simple. "Because you have to choose."

He watched her bite something back, then blink, as if maybe she'd forgotten where they were too. That fist, tucked away in her lap, tensed.

Later, he promised her silently. He'd deal with this later, whatever this was. When they didn't have an audience. When he could dig in a little bit and see what was happening in the middle of that winter storm he could see raging inside her. When he could figure out a way to kiss her again without being one more thing she had to recover from. Her lips flattened into a line, but she didn't argue further.

"I like it," Alex said when Hunter laid out his plan in all its quick and dirty simplicity. But they all looked at Zoe.

Who made them wait, of course. One beat, then another. That fist clenched hard, then she released it and folded both hands before her on the table.

"That might work," she said.

Grudgingly, Hunter thought, but she said it.

"It will work," Austin said with a short, bitter laugh. "Good job. He won't see it coming."

"I'm banking on it," Hunter said. "That and the fact his vanity won't allow any other outcome."

"Which puts him right where I want him." Alex grinned.

He met Hunter's gaze, and for the first time in years, Hunter didn't look away first. He didn't change the subject, crack a joke, put on his Hunter Talbot Grant III act and play the clown. He didn't pretend this man didn't know him—the real him he'd only just begun to understand he'd buried with Sarah.

Alex's grin broadened.

"I remember this Hunter," he said quietly, and then he reached over and clinked his glass against Hunter's. He looked at Zoe as if he had her to thank, then back toward Hunter as though they'd never been anything but close. "I like this Hunter. Welcome back."

He caught up with her at the corner outside, where Zoe was forging straight on through the intersection toward Union Square as if she couldn't get away from him fast enough.

"Are you running away from me?" Hunter demanded,

forgetting that he was trying not to upset her. The look she threw at him assured him that she wasn't making any such attempts.

"I am *walking,* not running," she said icily. "To a north-bound avenue, where I will hail a taxi. Then I will instruct it to drive the hell away from you."

"Fine," he said. It was two blocks to Park Avenue, the next northbound street. That gave him a window. He moved so he was walking in front of her, but turned back around to face her.

"Perfect," she said darkly. "I won't say that I hope you walk into a street sign and knock yourself unconscious, but I'm not going to do anything to prevent it, either. Just so you know."

"You should think about what I spent the past ten years doing for a living. I could walk the entire length of Manhattan backward without hitting a thing. I believe they call me *nimble.*"

She stopped walking. It was too cold, too dark on that side street, surrounded by brick buildings and concrete and the shoveled-high remains of the last snowstorm, but she didn't seem to care. So he didn't, either.

"That is not what they call you."

"What is this?" He had to clench his hands in his pockets to keep them to himself, and it was a battle to keep his voice pitched low. To remain—or anyway, appear—calm.

Zoe blew out a breath he could see against the frigid air, and then something swept over her. He could see it. Like a terrible quake. As if she was being shaken apart from the inside out.

But when she spoke, she whispered. And she wasn't looking at him.

"You're obviously disgusted," she said, not making any sense, though there was that darkness across her face and that vulnerable cast to her proud mouth, and he couldn't quite breathe. "Why can't you just admit it? Why play this sick game?"

"I'm not playing any games."

"I get it. I do. There's a reason I don't exactly advertise my sordid past—"

"Wait." He bent to make sure he was looking her straight in the face. "What are you talking about?"

"Don't pretend, Hunter." Her whisper had turned ragged. "Don't make it worse. All you see when you look at me is what he did. What *I* did. The taint of it." He was frozen solid in astonishment, and she kept talking, and he was sure she didn't realize that tears were rolling down her cheeks as she did, ripping into him with every track they left behind. "You couldn't keep your hands off me until you found out—"

"You were fucking *violated!*" he blazed at her, and she jumped, and he didn't care. Not when it was this important that she hear him. "You think I should grab you five seconds after you tell me something like that? You think my response to what you've been through should be trying to get in your pants?"

"Yes." Her voice cracked. "*Yes,* damn it."

"That's what—" He stopped and stared down at her, amazed. "Did you just say 'yes'?"

"It was a long time ago," she threw at him, as if she was trying to hurt him with every word. "I didn't die. I'm right here and I'm not *broken.*"

And Hunter understood she was talking to herself, not to him. Not really.

"You can't really believe—"

"I'm not going to beg you, Hunter, no matter how big that might make you feel. I shouldn't have to prove to you that I'm the same person I was two nights ago."

"Listen to me." It was an order, and he waited for her to stop. To look at him. To keep looking at him. "You like to play power games, and so do I. They're fun. But this has nothing to do with that."

"Don't kid yourself," she hissed at him. "Everything is a power game. *Everything.*"

"*I'm. Not. Him.*"

He didn't yell. He didn't have to yell. Those three words were their own brutal wind, howling around them, then down the urban canyon into the dark night. She flinched as if it had sliced straight through her, as if he'd cut her in half.

"Don't confuse me with that fucking degenerate again," he told her in the same voice, brooking no argument. "We're going to be very clear, you and me, about consent. Do you understand me? About what *you* want."

She shook, but he knew it wasn't from the cold this time.

She was fragile and fierce and *Zoe*, staring back at him from the middle of a nightmare she'd banished all by herself, and he thought he'd never loved another person like this in all his life. And he never would.

The truth of that rang in him, a long, low note, and changed everything.

But he still waited.

"I want to feel alive," she told him, her dark eyes too bright. Her voice was thick with that unmistakable crack in it, telling him everything. "Unbroken. Like he never ruined me in the first place."

"He never could," he whispered, shattered.

"Then why won't you…?"

But she didn't finish. Maybe she couldn't.

And this time, Hunter wasn't thinking about sex. He didn't care who was in charge and he wasn't thinking about playing games at all. He cared only about that look on her face, that matching hole in his heart. He was thinking only and entirely about Zoe.

He sank down to his knees again, right there on the frigid sidewalk, never taking his gaze from hers, giving her everything.

If she wanted it.

"I don't want you to beg," he told her, watching her face contort with the sobs she was fighting to keep back, the tears that had already betrayed her. "But I will, if you want. You can have anything you want from me, Zoe. All you have to do is ask for it."

She didn't ask. Instead, she moved forward. She wrapped herself around him, sinking her hands into his hair, and then kissed him.

Salt and sweet.

As if she already knew the answer.

As if he was a hero after all.

Zoe took him back to her apartment. Her sanctuary, where no one was ever allowed inside.

He stood in the center of her living room, starkly male, entirely Hunter. He seemed bigger than he had on the street—consuming all of the available oxygen without even seeming to try. The air around him seemed to *hum,* alive and electric, the way it always did. She felt too bright, too exposed, actually shaking with the effort to keep from flipping out—demanding he leave or, worse, collapsing in a jittery heap on her own floor. Instead, she pulled him down to the couch and climbed on top of him.

"This is consent," she whispered.

"That's all I need," he replied, and then, finally, he touched her. His warm, strong hands on her face, streaking down her back to cradle her hips. "You idiot."

"Don't call—"

"Zoe." He pulled her closer, and she was already melting. Already quivering. "Shut up."

And when she did, he claimed her.

He made her feel more than alive. White hot and glowing. He showed her—with his hands, his lips, his mouth and his fine body—that she was anything but ruined. That she could never be ruined. Again and again, until she was limp and he was hoarse and they could only hold each other, dazed.

When he'd made his point one more time, emphatically, she lay sprawled on top of him, bare skin to bare skin, stretched out across her bed. Breathing in that crisp, intoxicating scent of his, her head tucked in the crook of his neck. The closest she'd felt to *safe* in as long as she could remember—and she let herself pretend. In the dim light in her bedroom. In his arms.

That things like this could last. That this was real, when she knew better.

Tonight, she pretended.

"You okay?" he asked, and she realized she must have made some noise. She nestled closer, as if she was any other woman in the arms of her lover. As if that was possible.

"Demons exorcized," she murmured against his skin, and the funny thing was, in the glow that seemed to surround them then, she almost believed it.

And that was when Zoe understood what was happening to her. What had already happened. She hadn't imagined it *could* happen, so she'd never bothered to protect herself against it.

But it all made a dizzying, insane kind of sense. Her wild, ungovernable attraction to this man, when she'd been shut down to attraction for more than ten years. The fact she'd let him get to her the way he had, turning the tables on her in her own office. That he'd left a mark on her and she hadn't hated it. The fact she'd concocted a reason why she *had* to sleep with him. The fact she'd told him what had happened to her, and had only been hurt that he might not want her afterward.

Not that her secret was out. Not that she'd exposed herself. But that *he* might think less of her.

She'd been head over heels for Hunter Grant since the moment she'd clapped eyes on him.

How had she failed to recognize that until now?

"You've spent the past decade wallowing in self-pity," she said, the words tumbling out before she could think them through, sharp and accusatory.

But he was Hunter. So he only laughed.

"I have," he agreed, too mildly. "As you've helpfully pointed out approximately nine thousand times. A day."

She pushed herself up so she could frown at him. "All that fighting and carrying on, the bimbo parade—what was that?"

"My punishment," he said quietly, and the look in his eyes made her ache inside. "And not half of what I deserved."

She didn't look away. That long-ago December night reared up between them, so real she could almost reach out and touch it, however little she wanted to do such a thing. But Zoe knew more than her share about ghosts. How they festered. How they grew.

"Did you love her?"

She wasn't sure she'd meant to ask that. She wasn't sure she wanted to know.

Hunter blew out a breath, and suddenly, the space between them didn't feel like nearly enough. But she couldn't seem to move, and his arms were around her, tight, keeping her right where she was, tucked up against him as if she belonged there.

"I was eighteen when I met Sarah," he said after a moment. "Twenty-three when I lost her. We broke up and got back together a hundred times in those years. We were kids. If she'd lived, if she'd never gotten mixed up with Jason Treffen…" He sighed. "She was hungry and ambitious, passionate about everything, and I didn't have that kind of drive. I think she would have left me eventually for someone who did."

He smiled then, crooked and quiet.

"Yeah," he said. "I did. I really did."

He watched her then, and Zoe had the strangest falling sensation, as if everything was spinning all around and instead of it making her sick, she wanted nothing more than to let it sweep her away. The same way she had in her office, what seemed like such a long time ago.

At least now she knew why.

"I'm not Sarah."

She hadn't meant to say it like that, so stark and blunt. But she was unable to hide the panic, the desperate tide that threatened to drag her off into the dark. She felt as if she was crumbling into pieces right there in his arms, into ash and dust that could blow away into nothing at the first hint of wind.

"I know that," Hunter said quietly, his blue gaze never wavering from hers.

"You can't save me, either," she retorted, as if he'd argued with her.

There was a red thing inside her, hot and dangerous, and for the first time in years, she had no strategy. No plan. She just...*hurt*. She loved him and she knew better and she *hurt*.

"I don't need your white horse or your pity or whatever this is. I can't help you bring her back to life. Do you understand me?"

He shifted as if she'd sunk something sharp and deadly deep into his side. She let him smooth his palm over her cheek. She felt the heat of it, the strength, and God help her, but she'd never wished so deep or so hard that they were both other people.

That she was.

"I'm long past saving, Hunter," she said, a broken thread of sound, revealing everything. All of that mess inside her, still. The broken pieces, the shadows and the regrets and the terrible shame. "It can't be done."

"The thing is," he said. "I'm pretty sure you've already saved yourself."

His skin against her skin. His hand so gentle, so sure. His eyes so blue they took over the whole world, making her heart feel far too big for her chest, as if it might spill over, burst free, all through the apartment and down to the cold street outside, and she knew this couldn't last. She knew she couldn't let it. But here, now, she couldn't help herself.

She leaned into his hand. She let herself pretend.

"Not yet," she whispered.

After a few days of intense plotting, they were shown into a lush conference room on the highest floor of Treffen, Smith, and Howell by a deferential young woman whose carefully blank expression made Zoe's stomach hurt.

But it also fueled that deep, black anger inside her. Reminding her exactly why she was doing this. Exactly why she *had* to do this.

The last time she'd been in this building didn't bear thinking about, so she stood by the window and stared out at New York instead, gleaming there before her in the last of the afternoon light, looking so pretty and perfect and dusted in white, like a snow globe. As if nothing terrible could ever happen in the midst of all that gilt-edged urban beauty.

She wasn't aware that she'd made a noise until Hunter came to stand beside her, lending her his vast strength without even touching her. It hit her, then, how terribly she was going to miss him, miss this—but she couldn't let herself think about that now.

"You okay?" he asked.

She'd dressed to be more than okay. She'd dressed to kill, all sharp edges and royal blue, with that promise of payback in every line. Nothing submissive or subordinate or terrified about her. No mourning clothes. Like a sword. Like the avenging angel she'd made herself, just for this.

"No," she said. She glanced at him, taking solace in that gleam of pure blue the way she always did. "But I will be."

She was so close now. *So close.* Her revenge was within her grasp—and for the first time in all these years, it occurred to her to wonder what was waiting on the other side. What came after revenge?

But she heard the conference door open behind her, and she shoved the odd thought aside. She'd deal with it later.

"Isn't this a surprise?"

It was the same voice it had always been. Kind and fatherly, with all that malevolence beneath. The sound of it swept over Zoe like nausea the way it usually did, but she'd expected that. She waited for her knees to feel firm again, for her stomach to stop its pitch and roll, for the automatic wave of clamminess to subside.

Only then did she turn to face him.

Jason Treffen stood inside the glass doors of the conference room, smiling at her the exact same way he always had. That same trim, athletic figure in the same Italian sort of suit. The same hint of citrus-scented cologne around him that made her feel as if she was choking. Those same pale eyes of his, flat and cold. Reptilian.

Then he dismissed her with a single glance, looking at Hunter instead, as if Zoe was worthless. Invisible. Dirt unworthy of further notice.

But she'd expected that, too. She couldn't prevent the

wave of familiar, sickening self-loathing that dismissal triggered, as he'd meant it to do, the bastard. But she'd known it was coming, so it helped her keep her sharp smile in place while it crashed over her.

"Hunter," Jason said warmly. "I'm so happy you dropped by. It's been too long. I only have a few minutes tonight, but if you come by the house—"

"Like old times?" Hunter asked softly. Too softly. "Will we play some pool, drink some whiskey and laugh uproariously as you tell me how my life could be if I follow your shining example?"

Zoe watched Jason absorb that. The dark irony and leashed ferocity in Hunter's voice, at complete odds with the way he stood there next to her, one shoulder propped up against the wall as if he was wholly at his ease.

"Barring that, you're welcome to make an actual appointment to see me here." Jason's voice was soft, polite. "I always have time for you, Hunter."

That faint emphasis on the word *you*. As if it was embarrassing that Hunter had brought a filthy creature like Zoe here, but Jason was too well-mannered to mention it directly.

He was a master at these games. He always had been. On some level, she knew she'd learned more from him than she wanted to admit. But the benefit of that was he'd inadvertently taught her everything she needed to know to beat him.

As he was about to discover.

"Should he make that appointment with Iris?" Zoe asked, cool and unbothered, as if she was unaware of all the tensions and undercurrents that seethed in the room between them. "Wasn't that the name of the girl who brought us in here? I'm sure I saw you with her at a party not long ago, Jason. You remember."

There was a flicker in Jason's lizard eyes, then a different edge to that smile, and she knew she'd surprised him. Because she'd called him *Mr. Treffen* when he'd owned her and because this was the first time she'd initiated a conversation with him in a very long while.

But he looked at Hunter when he replied, "Iris is a legal assistant, not a secretary. She doesn't book my appointments."

Legal Assistant, Zoe thought then. Such a fussy title for such a deep, dark, damaging hole.

"Who does?" Hunter asked, in that deceptively light tone. He looked very large and very dangerous looming there, even in one of his absurdly expensive suits that had been tailored to make him look debonair instead of deadly. Like an uncaged animal pretending to be tame, New York spread out behind him like a great and glorious cape, and Zoe knew none of that was lost on Jason. "Book your appointments, I mean."

Jason's head tilted slightly to one side, as if he was seeing Hunter for the first time. "Did you really come to see me after all these years to discuss my support staff?"

"That depends on what kind of 'support' you think we're talking about. I'll give you a hint. It's not clerical."

Jason regarded him for a long, tense moment, then turned that slithery, horrible look on Zoe. And she forced herself to breathe, to really *look* back at this man, this vicious little man, and *see* him.

Not the savior she'd thought he was when she'd met him. Not the terrible monster he'd become. Not the tormentor he'd been all these years since, showing up when she least expected it, hurting her and threatening her and terrorizing her at his whim, for his own sick amusement.

Today, she'd chosen to come here. He had nothing to hold over her head. He was nothing but a man. A terrible man, still drunk on his own power. But only a man. And she was different, somehow, than she'd been before, all those other times he'd made sure to run into her. Fundamentally altered, because now that the initial punch of nausea had passed, he looked…smaller. Older. And next to a man the size and solid heft of Hunter, she could see that he was frail. Breakable.

So she met that awful gaze of his without flinching, and smiled.

"What is this?" Jason asked quietly, shifting his gaze back to Hunter. "I haven't seen you in a decade at least, and this feels a good deal like an attack. Especially given the company you're keeping."

"This isn't an attack," Hunter said in that same soft, dangerous way. "Believe me, you'll know it if I attack you."

"I expect this kind of bluster from Austin," Jason said. With a certain vicious precision. "He's always been a terrible disappointment, like so many sons are to their fathers. As I believe you have been to yours throughout your many escapades. It's a terrible cliché. But I'll confess, I did think better of you."

"I can't imagine why," Hunter said, and now he was smiling, because they'd planned for this, too. Austin had practically quoted his father in advance. "I've made it impossible for anyone to think better of me. All that unsportsmanlike behavior. All the temper tantrums out there on the field for all to see and judge. My complete lack of character is my singular adult achievement."

"Men like you aren't expected to have much character," Zoe agreed, in that arch way that kept her clients on edge, and appeared to have much the same effect on Jason.

"I don't really need it, do I?" Hunter grinned at her, and it warmed her. It reminded her that she wasn't alone here. That all of this was part of the strategy. That between them, and with Austin and Alex's help, they'd anticipated every one of Jason's moves. "I can let football do the talking. My throwing arm has always been pretty eloquent."

"And that's the beauty of it," Zoe replied, but she turned her gaze on Jason then. "Imagine if Hunter was to stumble into a character-building scenario. Become a new man in the eyes of the world. See the light, if you will, and in so doing, unburden himself about the terrible life he'd led up to that point."

"My own little road to Damascus," Hunter said, because he loved his saints, and Zoe had to bite back her smile.

Jason let out a sigh. "Zoe is a piece of ass, Hunter. You're supposed to fuck girls like this, not let them parade you around by your dick." He shook his head, as if he pitied Hunter. As if Zoe was radioactive. "This is embarrassing."

"Not yet," Zoe assured him. Was he aware that Hunter had turned to stone beside her? As if he was half a breath away from tossing Jason out the window? Or did he want to provoke that kind of violence—but he did, she realized. Of course he did. Then he could call himself the victim and sue. "We haven't even gotten to the good part."

Jason smiled, and it was deadly.

"What do you imagine you can do to me, you little bitch?" he asked in the same voice he'd always used. So kind, so genial, and that crushing darkness behind it. "Do you really think you can threaten me? *Me?* You must have forgotten everything I ever taught you."

"On the contrary," she said softly. "This is me using every last one of those lessons."

"Call her a bitch again," Hunter said conversationally, still so tense and furious behind that lazy exterior that it made the fine hairs on the back of Zoe's neck prickle, "and I'll break every single bone in your body."

But Jason only laughed. Still in that happy, fatherly way he always did, which made what came out of his mouth sound that much worse.

"If you'd been any kind of a man, maybe your girlfriend

wouldn't have had to prostitute herself, then kill herself to get away from you ten years ago. Should we talk about that?"

Zoe wanted to kill him then. Hunter didn't react, but she felt the lash of that blow, the sting of it, and the urge to draw Jason Treffen's blood hummed in her, electric and something like terrifying.

It was time to wrap this up. To be done with him.

"You're not going to do any more talking, Jason," she said with a grim satisfaction ten years in the making, feeling Sarah there with her and all the other girls he'd wrecked. Every one of them a part of this. "You've done quite enough. What you're going to do is leave this firm. Your days as a practicing lawyer are over. You're done."

There was a small, intense silence. Then Jason laughed again, a bigger laugh than before and nothing kind about it, and turned toward the door, dismissing her as if she was beneath his notice. Beneath contempt. Zoe waited until he had his hand on the door handle.

"And if you don't go of your own volition," she warned him with a great relish she made no attempt to hide, "you'll force me to have you kicked out."

That sparked the response she'd thought it would. Another laugh and then Jason turned back to look at her, cold and amused. Nothing but a nasty challenge in that flat gaze of his.

"I'd like to see you try."

Chapter Ten

Jason didn't actually say the word *bitch* this time but it hung there anyway, oily and vicious, polluting the air of the conference room, connecting with that reservoir of shame inside Zoe like a harsh kick to the belly.

She breathed through it, refusing to let him see he'd gotten to her.

"I was hoping you'd say that," Hunter said. He straightened then, and made a show of glancing at his remarkably expensive watch. "I'm meeting with the firm's equity partners in fifteen minutes. Given the number of lawsuits I generate, as I'm sure you know, I'm considered something of a cash cow. They like to keep me happy. All those billable hours and the personal fortune to keep on paying for them."

"Are you threatening to sue me?" Jason rolled his eyes. As if all of this bored him. "You can't simply wave your hands and create a lawsuit from thin air, Hunter. The courts tend to frown on that."

"I know I'm just a dumb jock," Hunter replied with the genial grin he'd trotted out a million times before, in any number of press conferences over the years, and Zoe loved him, deep and hard and frightening, "but I can still read. You remember the terms you drew up in the firm's partnership agreement, don't you? It takes a majority vote among equity partners to remove one of their own. I read it all by myself."

Jason wasn't smiling anymore. "That will never happen."

"Oh, it will," Zoe assured him. "I suspect the partners here are well aware of your little side business. I'm confident that none of them would like Hunter to make that business the cornerstone of his image rehabilitation tour, as discussing the firm's connection to your moonlighting as a pimp is unlikely to make the bar association happy. To say nothing of the firm's clientele, none of whom would enjoy having their relationship to a pimp speculated about in the press." Her lips crooked. "I'm just guessing."

"Who do you imagine would believe you?" Jason wasn't hiding anymore. The truth of who he was stamped on his twisted, furious, ugly face, and he took a step toward Zoe as if this was a decade back and he'd use his hands if he wanted. Some part of her wished he would. He'd find things had changed. "In case you've forgotten, Zoe, you're nothing but a whore. As I'll be more than happy to tell the entire world."

Hunter tensed again, harder, and his blue gaze went homicidal, but Zoe stepped forward, because it all came down to this moment. She'd fantasized about it for years. She'd schemed and she'd plotted and she'd gone over it in her head a thousand times. More.

And it was still better than she'd imagined.

"I'm not afraid of you any longer," she told the architect of her deepest, darkest shame. The monster beneath her bed. This small, pathetic man who preyed upon the weak—but she wasn't weak anymore. "I'm not the one who's about to receive a lifetime achievement award. I'm not the one who's built up such a shining reputation, based entirely on the perception that I'm good and kind and deeply committed to charity. I can have Hunter tell the world your entire sordid story, and what will it matter to me? No one will connect me to it, and even if they do, *you'll* still be tarnished." She leaned forward slightly. "Tainted. Forever."

"No one will listen to a word you say." But Jason didn't look as calm as he had before, or anything like amused.

"But they might listen to me." Hunter smiled then, and launched into his spiel, deeply earnest and sincere, as if he was playing it to the cameras. "The thing is, I'm changing my life. I've seen the light. I'm not a superstar football player anymore. I've let my family down and I've betrayed all my fans. I'm just a guy who's only good at one thing, and that's why I've decided to work as a football coach at Edgarton High. For free, until we win a state championship."

Jason's eyes narrowed at that, and Zoe took great pleasure in the beads of sweat that broke out across his forehead.

"You've heard of Edgarton, haven't you?" Hunter asked, conversationally. "Not a great place, or a great team, for that matter. I figure the state championship is a few years off. And, of course, that's where Sarah was from. But I'm sure you know that.'

"Sarah Michaels was a white-trash tramp," Jason said, harsh and quiet, one ugly slap after another. "From an entire family of born losers. I did her a favor. At least the kind of whoring she did for me, she got paid. She would have done much worse, and for much less, had she stayed in that dump."

"I bet those were her final thoughts," Zoe said, her voice a deliberately cool breeze in the tense room, her eyes fixed on the enemy. *Almost there. Almost.* "Gratitude for all your 'help.'"

She wondered if Sarah knew, somehow. If she was out there somewhere and could see what Zoe was doing. Sarah, who had been Zoe's first friend in New York City. Sarah, who had been Zoe's only friend once everything got so dark. Sarah, who had loved Hunter first, enough to leave him out of this nastiness. She flattered herself that Sarah would have supported this.

Zoe watched Jason breathe, more heavily than before. Then she watched the older man adjust his tie, smooth his hands down his jacket.

Nerves, she thought, with great satisfaction. Jason was betraying himself at last.

"You have ten minutes to decide if you're retiring or getting kicked out and then outed," she said into the simmering silence. "And I have to tell you, I don't care which you choose. I win either way." She caught Jason's eye, and held it, and it was almost worth all these years of suffering to see that little spark of uneasiness. Of something a good deal like fear. "I like to win, Jason. You should congratulate yourself. You taught me how."

Jason stood as still as a statue, and Zoe thought she could almost *hear* his twisted mind whirl, turning it over and over, looking for an exit strategy, a way to outplay them, a way to come out the winner. Zoe glanced at Hunter, who nodded almost imperceptibly in support, but she felt it bloom inside her, warm and bright like one of his smiles.

"Time's up," Hunter drawled after ten long, bitterly quiet minutes dragged by. He straightened and moved toward the door. "I have that meeting."

For a moment, Jason was silent, and Zoe wondered if she'd misjudged this, if they'd all miscalculated—

"I'll leave the firm," Jason gritted out, grudgingly, sourly, hatred heavy in each syllable, and distorting his face. His flat, pale eyes were the stuff of nightmares. But Zoe had been having this same nightmare for years now. She was over it. "But I'll give the media my own reasons for it."

"I don't care what you tell the media," she told him, not making the slightest attempt to hide her satisfaction. Her triumph. "Just so long as you leave this firm and all your victims behind. Because let's be clear. Your pimping days are over. You leave this firm and you say goodbye to your little ring. You lose everything except your good name. Just like we all lost everything the day you 'took an interest' in us."

Jason sneered at her, and she knew *that* face. She knew *this* man. This nasty little man, who was so vain he believed they'd actually leave him anything. *Just wait,* she thought.

"I wouldn't pop the champagne just yet, Zoe," he said. Murderously. "It will take more than that to best me. I'm adored by this entire city. This *country*. These little games of yours won't change that."

But then, Zoe was counting on that. They all were.

"Time to talk to your partners," she said, and then she smiled, big and bright and she didn't care if he saw it, because it was over. It was finally over.

She was free.

She was free, and that made her foolish. Sentimental and soft.

Or maybe that was Hunter.

That first night, she couldn't help herself. Jason quit the law firm as they'd told him he must, and she and Hunter had walked out of that loathsome building together, stunned. Victorious. They'd been in a taxi together before she could think better of it, and he'd pulled her into his lap, kissing her again and again, as if she was a marvel.

How could she do anything but fall into the man who had shared this exquisite, hard-won triumph with her? How could she keep herself from enjoying him?

Just this one last time, she told herself as the cab lurched its way south. As Hunter kissed her, deep and slow and long, as if he was content to do nothing else. As if there *was* nothing else. Just his mouth on hers, the dance of tongues and teeth and longing, his hand at the back of her head and that hard body of his below her, around her.

As if it could never end, when she knew better.

And in the morning, Jason Treffen was all over the news, puffed up and magnanimous, talking about how he'd felt it was time he left his law practice to better dedicate himself to his charity work.

The unsubtle subtext was: *Aren't I the most wonderful man alive?*

"That was not exactly what I had in mind when contemplating his downfall and disgrace for the past ten years," Zoe said, standing in the kitchen she'd have thought Hunter never used, stealing bites of his bagel.

She was wearing nothing but one of Hunter's T-shirts. It fell low on her thighs and made her feel small and cherished, like a beloved girlfriend, and she knew better than that. She knew better than the kind of intimacy it suggested, or the way he grinned when he swatted at her hand, as if they were those kinds of people. *Normal.* Something like right.

But that sick, sentimental part of her wanted to feel what it was like. No matter how badly it was going to hurt later.

"He'll get his," Hunter said, standing there in all his lean glory on the other side of the center island. He took a swig from his coffee and then pointed the mug at her. "I promise you that. Alex has been waiting his entire life to take Jason down. Didn't you see that one reporter ask if there was trouble in paradise—the divorce, leaving the firm, changing his entire life in a very short span of time?"

"I saw Jason handwave it all away by acting like all of those things were his very own idea," she replied darkly. "Mostly because he's so *good* and *loving* and *moral* and *righteous*. And I saw them eat it up the way they always do."

"There are cracks everywhere he looks, Zoe," Hunter said softly. "It's only a matter of time. You've destroyed him. It's not going to take much for that facade of his to shatter."

And he was so open, so *bright,* that guilt swamped her—and he saw it. He saw everything. For a moment that shrewd blue gleam made her breathless.

"Are you going to tell me what's wrong?" he asked.

It was harder than it should have been to smile. To fight that tide of misery back, to force herself to look the way she should after the night they'd had. After what they'd done. *Happy,* at the very least. Whatever the hell that was.

"What could possibly be wrong?" she asked, but she could see her light tone didn't fool him at all.

And then the doorman called up from downstairs to tell him he had a delivery, saving her from having to pretend any further, because Austin had sent Hunter flowers.

Epic flowers. Delicate tulips and all manner of lilies, orchids and succulents and plump, round chrysanthemums. Explosions of hydrangeas in blues, purples, pinks and whites. When the parade of deliverymen finally left, Hunter's apartment was filled with them. They stood in the once-sterile great room, now exploding with so many colors it was almost dizzying, surrounded by all the competing scents.

"Does he think he missed your funeral?" Zoe asked.

And Hunter laughed. Real laughter, delighted and intoxicating, and it shook her. She could see, suddenly, who he might have been. Who he would be again, once all of this was behind him. If Sarah Michaels had gone to a different firm after college. If he'd spent the past decade doing something other than mourning out loud and in public like that, so everyone could see and hate him the way he hated himself. If she'd never hunted him down and dragged him into her orbit, back into this terrible mess.

Sarah had loved him enough to let him go. How could Zoe do anything less?

But even then, even when it was so clear what she had to do, she couldn't bring herself to do it.

Because he picked her up and pulled her legs around his waist, and by the time he put her down again, she'd forgotten everything but the fierce joy of his hands on her body. The slide of his gorgeous torso against hers.

He kissed her mouth, her cheekbones, her eyelids, as if she was the celebration. His perfect mouth moved into an intent sort of smile that made her blood seem sluggish and hot in her veins. So she lifted herself up on her toes, wrapped her arms around his wide shoulders and kissed him back.

Again and again, until there was no telling who was kissing who, when it was only heat and desire and *this*. Them.

This one last time.

Zoe explored him, taking it slow. Imprinting him onto her fingertips, her lips. Making it last, so she'd have it to remember. She stripped the clothes from his body, tasting every bit of hard, smooth skin she discovered along her way.

And she didn't care that she was barefoot and decidedly rumpled, her hair hanging all around her, because he lay her down on his pure white couch and he moved over her as if she was the most beautiful woman he'd ever seen. And even though she knew better, she let herself believe it. Just for now. She poured it into her kiss. She let him see it on her face.

She couldn't seem to help herself.

Hunter nipped at her lower lip even as his hardness nudged her center, insistent and demanding where she was molten and soft, teasing her. Making them both shudder.

He said her name and then he thrust into her, hard and deep. Then they were rolling, and she was on top. He sat up, too, his hands at her waist, and it was her turn to move, to ride him, to tease him, to take him deep inside her and then pull back, to writhe and dance them both to that edge—

"I love you," he said, as he threw her straight into that fire.

And Zoe shattered all around him, into so many pieces she knew she'd never be the same again, especially when he said it again as he followed.

But when she could breathe again, the words he'd said still echoed inside her—like a wish, like a prayer—and she knew it was time.

Past time.

"Come on," he said into the crook of her neck, those possessive hands still clasped to her, still holding her against him. He was still deep inside her, and she was so miserable it felt like being wrenched apart, deep within. Like some kind of organ failure. "I need a shower."

Zoe pushed herself away from him, and it was much harder than it should have been to sit up. To let go of him. To climb up off that couch.

To do this thing she didn't want to do, but had to do. She knew she had no choice.

She never, ever had a goddamned choice.

"I'm going," she said, pushing the words out hard. Fast. "I have to go."

Because she wasn't sure she'd say them, otherwise. Hunter was the most tempting thing she'd ever seen, stretched out on that couch of his, the stark whiteness of it calling only more attention to what a perfect specimen he was. As if he'd been carved from marble, gilded in bronze. His eyes were still bluer than all the California days she'd ever seen, and they were lazy on hers now. Indulgent.

"Okay," he said. He didn't understand. "Where are you going? Also, you're naked."

"This is over," she told him, aware that she sounded too stiff. Too awkward. "I've wanted revenge for over a decade, and we did it. But there's no reason to continue this..." But she couldn't think what to call it, and he was sitting up with that narrow look on his face, and she couldn't seem to pull in a full breath. "I want to thank you, of course."

"Don't."

"Don't thank you?"

"Don't do this."

Zoe could tell he understood then, in the way he stared at her as if she was killing him. The way his voice came out, too dark and too rough.

"Besides," she said, making herself sound cheerful, though she was afraid it came out psychotic, "you have the attention span of a gnat. Everyone knows it. I think you deserve a starlet or two after all your hard work, don't you?"

"And don't pretend this is about me."

Zoe couldn't look at him anymore. She found the royal blue dress she'd worn to the law firm in a heap at the bottom of the spiral stair, and felt better once she'd pulled it on. She'd taken down a monster in this dress. She could survive this last battle, too.

"I love you," he said again.

But that was impossible.

"No," she said, clipped and certain. "You don't."

She hadn't seen him move, and now he was standing there right in front of her, pissed off and hurt and she hated this. She hated that she couldn't reach out the way she wanted to do. She couldn't have this. She couldn't have *him*.

Zoe was furious with herself that she'd pretended otherwise, when she knew. She'd always known.

"You can run out of here naked if you want," Hunter

gritted at her. "I won't stop you. I won't make you do something you don't want to do, Zoe. Ever. I meant that." His face went fierce, and that made her feel soft and tremulous inside. "But don't you fucking tell me what I feel."

"You don't know what he did to me," she threw at him. "You have no idea what I did. How many times I did it. What happened to me."

"You did what you had to do to survive," he said flatly. "Do you really think I'm going to blame you for that?"

"Maybe not now. But you will. It's inevitable."

"There isn't a single thing you could tell me that would make me want you less," Hunter told her, his voice hoarse and those blue eyes so intent on hers. "Not one thing."

"People say that. Then they hear things they can't get past."

"Who are you talking to?" He chided her gently. "You know some of the things I've done. There were whole tabloids dedicated to them."

"You did those things *by choice*."

"Which makes me an asshole. And makes you a—"

"Victim? Survivor? Whore? It's all the same thing. Marked and changed and different from everyone else. *Ruined*."

"Beautiful," he contradicted her, soft and fierce. The way he looked at her felt like a touch, falling everywhere his gaze did. Each cheekbone. Each eyebrow. "Strong. Sexy. Gorgeous." Her forehead. Her mouth. "Not ruined, Zoe. You couldn't be ruined if you tried."

"Hunter." She loved him. It was why she had to leave before he saw the things she wanted most to hide. Especially from him. "I can't do this."

"You can't or you don't want to?" he asked. She saw the vulnerability in him then, and it ripped through her, tearing her up.

"Both."

His hands were on his hips and he let out a long breath, as if he was winded. She wanted to touch him again. She wanted to hold him. But if she didn't leave now, she knew, she'd fall apart in front of him, and she couldn't do that. She owed him this. A goodbye he could believe, so he wouldn't chase after her. As Sarah had done for him a decade ago.

So he could live a life outside Jason Treffen's shadow. Zoe might have exacted her revenge on the man, but he'd still destroyed her. There was no changing that. Hunter could be free of that, at last. She wanted that for him. For one of them.

She started for the door, but she couldn't help stopping when he called her name, as if her body was conspiring against her.

"I love you," he said again, with even more of that painful ferocity, as if it was tearing him apart. "That's not going to change just because you don't want to believe it. It's never going to change."

"You love a ghost," Zoe said. She turned back to face him and hated herself when she trembled at that look in his beautiful eyes, on his perfect face. "She died ten years ago, Hunter, and I'm not her replacement."

"I can tell the difference." That was anger there, mixed with the hurt, and that was better. She told herself that had to be better. "She took herself out. You didn't. You fought. You're nothing like her."

She jerked her head at the flowers surrounding them, like a wall of fragrance. Like her own wake.

"Your friends lost her, too," she said. "You should give them a chance."

"This is not about Sarah, and it's not about them," he threw at her. "How stupid do you think I am?"

That stung. "I don't think you're stupid at all."

"Then stop treating me like a dumb jock. I know how you feel about me. And I know how much that must terrify you."

She could see how he fought himself, his hands in fists at his side. She knew exactly how hard it was for him to keep from coming to her, because she felt it, too. Need and longing coursed through her, clamoring inside her, demanding she not do this—

But the fear was worse. And she knew she couldn't do it again. She couldn't trust *herself*. If she loved something, if she trusted it, she was wrong every time. Her grandparents. Jason. Hunter deserved better than that. Than her.

And she knew that no matter what he said, she was broken beyond repair. Broken where it counted. He didn't want that. He couldn't. He wanted that girl he'd loved a long time ago, who'd left him before he'd discovered what she was, and hadn't lived to let all of that darkness turn her into…this.

"You took him down," Hunter said quietly. So fiercely that it beat inside her like its own harsh drum. "Don't let him take this."

But that was the point, wasn't it? It was too late. It always had been. Jason Treffen had taken the best part of her a decade ago. What she had left was good, and it was hers, but it wasn't what she might have been. It wasn't what Hunter deserved.

She loved him enough to see that.

Zoe smiled at him, but it felt like acid, and he took it like a punch. Hard and to the gut. She saw him flinch, and that only made her hate herself more.

"This is the right thing to do," she said.

"Are you trying to convince you or me?" he threw back at her.

And so she did the only thing she could: she walked away.

Hunter drove out to Edgarton the next day, hours earlier than the usual time he showed up for his makeshift practices. He waited until classes were in session before he walked into the school, not wanting to cause any kind of commotion. Not wanting anyone to see him until he got what he came for.

The security being as nonexistent as ever in Edgarton High, it didn't take him long to find Jack's classroom simply by walking the halls until he happened upon it. Jack looked different standing at a blackboard. He stood taller, was more engaging. Because he knew who he was when it involved math, Hunter thought. Just as Hunter knew who he was with a football in his hand. It was what he could do, what he was good at.

He might have been walking around without a heart since Zoe had ripped it out and flattened it right there in front of him, but he could still throw a football. He supposed there was magic in that, somewhere. And as he'd wasted enough of his life feeling sorry for himself, he might as well use it.

He stood in the hall until Jack glanced out and saw him, then he indicated the other man should come out and speak to him with a simple lift of his chin. Jack look startled. Hunter heard his voice rise, ordering textbooks opened and talking stopped, with the supreme confidence of a man who expected to be obeyed in his domain.

Jack closed the door behind him gently as he stepped through it, and cleared his throat a few times as he moved into the hall. He looked around as if surprised to see that Hunter was alone—or, Hunter reflected, maybe he simply wasn't comfortable looking Hunter in the eye. That made him feel like an ass, so he made an effort to adjust his stance, to ratchet back that unconscious level of aggression he suspected he broadcast automatically. Maybe he always had.

Maybe that was why she'd left—but he stopped himself. He knew it wasn't. Just as he knew that he had to let her choose. He'd promised her that he'd never force her into anything. He couldn't rescind that promise because things hadn't gone the way he'd wanted them to go. That would make him no better than Jason.

But Jack didn't relax. As if the man who commanded that classroom so easily was only a role he played. And suddenly, shockingly, Hunter realized where he'd seen that before. *In himself.* In the dumb jock role he'd played for his more in-tellectual friends, the whole world, all the way back to the ruthlessly smart Sarah, who he'd believed cheated on him with the most intelligent man they knew: Jason. He'd been playing his clown role ever since.

And Zoe was the only one who hadn't bought it.

That insight stunned him so completely that for a mo-ment he hardly knew where he was.

"I knew this day would come," Jack was saying, and his rueful tone snapped Hunter back into the here and now. "It's okay. I'll think of something to tell them."

Hunter only stared at him and Jack cleared his throat again, shifting from one foot to the other.

"Do I make you uncomfortable?" Hunter asked. Jack look startled, but then he grinned.

"Only in the sense that you're built like a tank, and could crush me with one hand," he said. "Maybe two fingers? But I wouldn't say that makes me uncomfortable. Reasonably cautious, perhaps."

Hunter found he was biting back a grin. "Caution is good."

"They won't thank you, so I will," Jack said after a moment, his own grin fading. He straightened, squared his narrow shoulders. "What you've done here made a difference. I know what kind of prospects these kids have, and they do, too. They'll carry this with them for a long time." He took a breath, and met Hunter's gaze straight on. "No one in Edgarton will ever think you're anything but a hero, Hunter. *That's* who you are. Not that story they tell on *SportsCenter,* stitched together from disgruntled old teammates and too much envy. I hope you know that."

It took Hunter a very long time to catch his breath against that sudden pressure in his chest, that mighty fist around his head, making him think he might burst wide open, betray himself.

"I'm not a hero," he said gruffly, when he thought he could speak. "Not by a long shot. Ask anyone." Ask Zoe, who he couldn't save. Not from Jason. Not from herself. Or Sarah, who he'd never tried to save. "I only came here to make myself look good. It was a cynical manipulation from the start."

Jack's gaze didn't waver on his.

"Maybe that's why you came the first time," he said evenly. "But that's not why you kept coming back."

Hunter didn't know how to handle this moment, stripped bare and so unvarnished. He nodded once, harsh and abrupt, and told himself that was enough.

"I'll say your goodbyes for you," Jack said gently, swallowing hard as he turned for his classroom door. "Take care of yourself, Hunter."

Which was when Hunter finally understood what was happening.

"Jack," he said, before the other man could open that door, before he could think too much about what he could or couldn't say. "Why do you think I'm here?"

Jack turned back to face him. "Uh. You're leaving? I'm touched you came in person, really—"

"I'm not leaving," Hunter barked out, unduly aggressive, because he was afraid that anything else would turn unacceptably soft in a hurry. "I want your job."

It was Jack's turn to stare.

"My...?" He half turned toward the classroom, but then stopped and shook his head. Then smiled, wide. "You don't mean my math classes."

"No," Hunter said quietly. And his own smile felt different then, as if it was new. As if it belonged to that man Jack had described, who Hunter didn't recognize as himself. But he wanted to be that man, after all these years. At long last. He wanted it badly, more badly than he wanted to admit. For these kids. For Zoe, if she ever found her way back to him. Maybe even for himself. "I don't mean math."

He was headed toward the school exit some time later when he heard the sound of running feet behind him, hard against the old linoleum flooring. He turned, and realized as he did, as he identified the figure hurtling toward him at breakneck speed, that he probably should have expected this.

"Listen, kid—" he started, but Aaron was vibrating and out of control. Pissed, Hunter saw, and utterly reckless with it.

"I don't give a shit what you do," the kid threw at Hunter, getting in his face, his own twisted with wild emotion. *Loss,* Hunter thought, *and disappointment.* He'd seen them often enough when people looked at him. He knew them well. "It's not like I was a fan of yours before you showed up, and now? It turns out you're even more of a loser than I thought you were."

"Aaron." He told himself to be gentle. Kind.

Both things he wasn't any good at, of course, or he'd have been someone else.

"The truth is, *you* suck," the kid gritted out, and Hunter recognized that, too. The howl of pain beneath the angry words. The hurt that spoke of other, harder abandonments. Of much deeper losses, the kind that never quite went away. "We didn't need you showing up here, trying to make yourself feel better about your own shitty life, driving your slick car around and acting like you're better than everyone else—"

"Are you talking about football? Because I actually am better than everyone else. In Edgarton anyway. That's not my ego, kid. That's fact."

"Go to hell."

"I've been there," Hunter said, studying Aaron's flushed

face, his bunched-up hands at his sides, that shattered look in his dark eyes. It was like looking in some kind of twisted mirror, and it confirmed that he'd made the right decision here. That no matter what happened with all the rest of the things he had in motion, *this* was the right thing. This kid, so desperate to be a man and so uncertain how to go about it, was why. He mattered. *This* mattered. "I can't recommend it."

Aaron said something even more foul, and Hunter laughed. *Gentle* and *kind* wouldn't have worked on him at any point during his downward spiral, and he'd been raised on a steady diet of privilege and financial support. Why try them on a kid like Aaron, who'd probably assume they were a trick?

Besides, he couldn't do it. He didn't know how.

"Aaron," he said sharply then. "Shut up." Aaron glared at him, fury and attitude sparking from his skin, clouding up the air around them like a testosterone mushroom cloud, but Hunter saw beneath it. "I'm your new coach. Officially."

The principal had practically wet himself at the notion, assuring Hunter that they could expedite his hiring through the Edgarton School Board, such as it was, especially as Hunter was perfectly happy not only to take the lowest salary they could offer him by law, but to donate three times that amount back into the school system—to the brand-new athletic budget.

Because it had occurred to him after Zoe left that he could actually do what he'd told Jason he was going to do only to mess with the other man's head, to push him where they'd needed him to go. It had occurred to him that more than that, he *wanted* to do it. That he might even be good at it.

He didn't share that part with Aaron. He only stared at him as the kid's breathing changed from that wild, angry panic into something more manageable.

"I'm not going to be at practice for the next few days," Hunter continued evenly. Because he had to get used to that hollow place Zoe had left inside him before he unleashed it on these kids. And because he'd decided he should drive up to Boston and offer an overdue apology to his long-suffering parents while he was feeling so benevolent and bruised. "But you better be. And believe me when I tell you that when I return, your attitude needs to be adjusted. One hundred percent. Do you understand me?"

Aaron looked like the kid he was then, sagged there against the wall, and Hunter's chest felt a little bit too tight. Maybe more than a little.

As if he'd been frozen, too, all these years, and Zoe had melted all that ice away.

"I understand," Aaron said after a minute, and Hunter nodded.

"If you don't, you'll figure it out in push-ups and extra laps," he said darkly. "Count on it."

He hesitated a moment, then reached over and clapped Aaron on his shoulder, feeling the boy's breath rush out of his body. And then he walked away, back toward his car

and New York and all the other things he needed to do—
but not before he saw Aaron grin, wide and hard and kind
of painful at the floor between his feet, as if he was afraid
someone would see and take it from him.

But not too afraid. Not enough to stop.

Chapter Eleven

The world didn't stop turning just because *her* world had shifted off its axis, Zoe found.

There was still her work, which she told herself she'd never enjoyed more. She sorted out a politician's unfortunate sexting scandal, tutored a debutante on how best to counteract her reputation as an airhead in order to raise money for a charity close to the heart no one knew she had, and started initial talks with a band who wanted to make a splash with their first new album in ages.

She'd lived more than thirty years without Hunter Talbot Grant III. Why should a week without him seem so empty? This was the good life, she told herself as one day turned into the next, and she was perfectly fine. *Perfectly fine.* This was what it looked like when Jason Treffen was neutralized and she could simply...live.

Except Hunter refused to disappear the way she'd assumed he would.

He'd showed up for his usual meeting a few days after

that last wrenching scene in his apartment, shocking her. She hadn't been ready to see him. She hadn't been ready to watch that low, easy saunter of his, or see that cool, assessing gleam in his blue eyes. He'd walked into her office as if he owned it, then thrown himself down on her couch with all the nonchalance in the world.

She hadn't been prepared for how much it still hurt. So much she had to sit down at her desk, for fear her legs would betray her.

"What are you doing here?" she'd asked him, in some shaky rendition of her usual businesslike tone.

"It's Tuesday," he'd said, as if that was an explanation. When she'd only stared at him, his mouth had crooked slightly. "I have a standing Tuesday meeting. I require that much consultation about my image, so damaged is it. You said so yourself."

"Jason left the law firm," she'd said, helplessly. Something had rocked through her as he stared back at her, vicious and extraordinarily painful.

"I know. I was there."

"This isn't necessary any longer."

There'd been a gleam in those blue eyes of his that had made her feel hollowed out. Raw.

"Do I strike you as rehabilitated, Zoe?" he'd asked, more dangerous than she'd ever seen him.

Which was when she'd admitted to herself that she didn't want him coming to her for his *image*. That she'd looked up, seen him in her doorway, and hoped against hope that he'd decided not to take no for an answer—

But he'd promised her he'd never do that.

She'd been appalled at herself, that she should want him to do it anyway. At the sad truth that she was still so weak.

And worse, she'd been certain Hunter had known it.

"Let me get Daniel," she'd thrown back at him. "He'll be taking over your account."

"Of course he will. With a song in his heart, I'm sure."

"If you have a problem with that," she'd said tightly, "there are a number of other public relations firms in the city that I'd be happy to recommend to you."

But Hunter had only smiled.

And Zoe had to live with that, because making the scene she wanted to make would expose her too completely and she suspected Hunter knew it. She had to take it home with her to an apartment that had always seemed perfectly comfortable before, and now felt empty.

As if he'd left holes behind when she'd left him. In everything.

And then Daniel, who knew nothing about Jason Treffen or the deliberate way they'd been keeping Hunter's reimagined image under wraps to force him into the corner where they wanted him, went ahead and treated Hunter like any other client.

Which meant Zoe suddenly saw him everywhere. In the tabloids, which screamed about his romantic assignation in a horse-drawn buggy through Central Park, only to shamefacedly announce that no, in fact, the new woman in Hunter Grant's life was his little sister, Nora. In the papers, which showed him at art events and charity functions, smiling and *almost* avoiding the cameras.

He was doing every single thing she'd told him he should do, but she refused to let that ignite within her like hope. He was doing it because she was good at her job, and what she'd suggested worked. That was all.

She told herself it couldn't possibly be anything else. That she didn't *want* it to be anything else.

"I thought you hated Hunter Grant," Zoe said after she and Daniel had gone over a few figures one afternoon and he didn't rage about Hunter even once. Not even the smallest bitter aside. "Yet you seem to be working past that."

"It turns out he's not that bad," Daniel said, and he even smiled. "I'm as surprised as anyone, but I kind of like the guy."

It was beneath her, Zoe told herself after he left her office, to view that as some kind of personal betrayal.

Daniel chose a very popular comedy show that focused on the news for Hunter's first brand-new-image interview, letting Hunter go on the show to allow them to make fun of him. A lot of fun of him. Merciless fun of him, as was their trademark.

Hunter even joined in.

And then at one point he grinned as if he was embarrassed and rubbed a hand over his head, saying almost bashfully that it was actually *his* honor to see if he could teach his new students a little love of the game—and, God willing, better manners—

"So, you're a 'do as you say, not as you do' kind of guy?" the host asked. Hunter shrugged, and then laughed. At himself.

"I think I'm more of a 'if you can't be a good example then you'll serve as a horrible warning' kind of a guy," he said. "And I think I've made it pretty clear that being any kind of a good example is off the table. Making me six feet and then some of a harsh warning."

The way he laughed then, long and deep, like a shower of light that bathed her in brightness where she sat all alone in her bedroom, told Zoe she'd made the absolute right decision to walk away from him, for all the reasons she'd told him and the ones she hadn't told him, too.

But it was killing her.

And Zoe told herself that she'd been dead long enough. It was time to live, no matter what it cost. To stop hiding the way she'd promised herself she would, no matter the collateral damage.

To *do something,* because she didn't think she could spend another moment pretending she was fine when she doubted she'd be anything like fine again, as long as she drew breath.

As long as he did.

Zoe didn't let herself think too much once she'd decided what she'd do.

It was easy to find out Hunter's schedule from Daniel's

calendar, and easier still to sweep past the usual gatekeep-ers into the benefit event held in a cavernous art gallery in SoHo.

What was difficult was walking up to Hunter when she saw him standing near the bar in a loose group of well-dressed beautiful people, among them his sister and Zair, her former client, the only one of her clients whose nondis-closure agreements had stumped her own lawyer.

If she could take down Jason Treffen in the very same of-fice where he'd destroyed her so long ago, she told herself as she eyed that gleaming little knot of people, Hunter the brightest by far among them, she could do this.

But he looked up and saw her from across the room, his gaze searing into her as if he'd been expecting her, and it was the longest, hardest walk of her life.

"Zoe," Zair murmured when she approached, in his cul-tured, British-tinged voice that was as dark and as danger-ous as he was. "What a pleasure."

Austin greeted her with a smile, his arm around a pretty girl who looked familiar. Alex grinned, as if they were all friends. When Zoe thought that really, they were Hunter's friends the way they were meant to be, and she was just…a problem she should have kept away from this. From him.

But she couldn't do it. She couldn't make herself do it any longer, and while she knew what that made her, she couldn't seem to stop this.

"I wasn't aware you were attending this gala," Hunter said after a moment, when it was clear she wasn't going to say anything to him. His gaze was blue and knowing and it almost took her down to her knees. She almost let it. "Do you know my sister? Nora, this is Zoe Brook. She manages my PR."

Zoe smiled, shook hands with his pretty, innocent sister, who had no idea who she was touching, and wanted to die.

"Can I talk to you?" she asked him, with an urgency she wasn't sure she managed to conceal.

Hunter arched a brow. "Here? But the dancing's just started, and I wouldn't want to abandon my sister to all these vultures."

He was teasing her, she thought. This was ripping her apart where she stood, this was harder than she'd imagined anything could be, and he was teasing her.

"Leave Nora to me," Zair said with a certain dark gallantry that would have piqued Zoe's interest, had she been capable of such things at a moment like this.

"Nora is a fully functioning human being, thank you," Nora herself interjected, but Zoe couldn't tear her eyes away from Hunter, and he only laughed.

And then it was a blur. He led her across the great room, dodging all the people who wanted to stop him to say a few words, smiling and laughing as if he was having the time of his life—

Until he ushered her through a door into a smaller gallery, blocked off from the main event with canvases stacked three-deep against the wall.

And when he looked at her then, she saw he wasn't happy or carefree at all.

The blue in his eyes burned her. His mouth was in that flat, hurt line she remembered much too well, and he looked at her as if the things he wanted to say to her were fighting to get out.

But he didn't say a word. He waited.

"You seem to spend a lot of time with your sister these days," she said in a panic, because she didn't know how to do this.

"Someone once pointed out to me that she is, in fact, fairly impressive for a twenty-four-year-old."

Then he continued to do nothing at all but watch her.

He looked too good. He looked like Hunter. He wore a sleek dark suit tonight, and oozed power. And safety. And the look he was giving her made her heart thud too hard inside her.

And he deserved so much better and she wasn't sure she cared.

"You paid the firm for our—for Daniel's services," she said.

"Is that why you're here? To discuss accounting?"

"I told you it was pro bono," she gritted out.

"I pay my bills, Zoe. Always. You can take that as a meaningful metaphor if you like."

She thought he might say something else then, but he still merely stood there, big and forbidding. Waiting. He shoved his hands in the pockets of his trousers and his blue eyes bored into her, and she knew she had to do this.

Before she talked herself out of it. Before she lost her nerve.

It was the most selfish act of her life, and he was looking at her as if he knew it, and she understood that if she was any kind of good person or ever wanted to be, if she cared about him at all, she would turn around and leave him. That doing that before had been the right thing to do. *She knew it.*

But she couldn't bring herself to move.

"Hunter," she whispered, trembling as if she was freezing cold and more scared than she'd ever been in her life, "I think I've made a terrible mistake."

He didn't crack. He didn't even bend.

"You think or you know? And which mistake are we talking about, Zoe? I'll need specifics."

She shook as if he'd hit her, and Hunter wanted nothing more than to go to her. To pull her close, feel the press of her against him, assure himself she was *real* and *here, safe* instead of standing in front of him with all of that fear so stark and clear on her pretty face, as if she was terrified of him.

Of *this,* he figured, and he couldn't make it easy on her. He couldn't help her. She had to do it herself.

"This isn't easy," she whispered.

His brave, beautiful Zoe, with nightmares in her eyes.

"Tell me one thing that is," he said as if he didn't give a shit. "One thing that matters that's even a little bit easy."

"Does this matter?" she asked, and the vulnerability in her voice then almost made him relent—but he couldn't do it.

Not if he wanted everything from her. And he did. This was why he'd waited.

"I don't have time for whatever game this is," he said shortly.

"This isn't a game—"

"Then stop playing," he bit out. "I told you I loved you and you walked out on me. Don't fish around to figure out *my* feelings. Tell me what you want. *Ask me,* Zoe, and you just might get it."

It was a deliberate echo of that night on the street, and her cheeks bloomed with color, shame or heat or regret, he didn't know which. But it was better than that awful look on her face the day she'd left him. It was better than the frozen way she'd looked at him since. It was better than blue-gray eyes filled with nightmares.

And she was standing here in front of him, clearly in the grip of some intense emotion, so all of this was better, no matter what happened next.

"You deserve better," she intoned, soft and something like wounded and not like any version of Zoe he knew. "Sarah loved you enough to leave you, and I tried to do the same, Hunter. You can be free of this, and you should be. Of the stain of what Jason did to her. To me. What we did to survive it—or not."

He didn't trust himself to speak, so he waited, watching

her. Her eyes were dark like rain, and her face was drawn. She stood with her hands clasped in front of her, like something out of a submissive fantasy playbook, and his hands bunched into fists, because it wasn't her. He didn't know what the hell this was, what was taking her over and making her play it out like this, but it wasn't the Zoe he knew. There was no fire. No power. No *Zoe*.

She swallowed hard. "I'm sorry," she whispered. "But I can't seem to stay away from you, even though I know I should. Even though I know that it's the best thing for you."

"So you came here to—what?" he bit out, hardly recognizing his own voice. She frowned as if she thought he might bite her, and not in a fun way. As if he was made of fangs and she'd been bitten before. It pissed him off.

"You told me you'd make me beg," she said. "This is me begging."

And she sank down onto her knees, right there in front of him, graceful and somehow frail despite the beautiful dress she wore, that clung to her in a dark shade of green and made all of her curves look even more edible than usual.

But all Hunter saw was her bowed head, her unnatural stiffness, her completely out-of-character behavior. What *was* this? It pissed him off even more.

"I owe you at least this much," she told him quietly. Almost demurely.

And suddenly, he got it.

"Is this because you think I like saints?" he asked drily,

and liked it when she tensed at his tone. "You thought you'd come out and play the martyr for me?"

She jerked her head up and there was a spark in her gaze he recognized, and he felt it the way he might have felt another woman's kiss. His Zoe. *His,* beneath this weird act of hers that he understood now, even if it broke his heart.

He wanted her back, all of her, no matter whose heart had to break to get there.

"I don't know what you mean," she said, and she ducked her head down again, and this sucked. He liked *playing* power games with women who weren't actually doormats. With this one in particular, because that was what was hot: the fact that the Zoe he knew was never meek or a supplicant. The Zoe he knew wanted him with a ferocity that matched the way he wanted her. This was something out of those dark things in her head, and he wanted nothing to do with it.

"I hate doormats," he drawled. "Sorry. Though you can crawl around if you want. Who knows? Maybe that will change my mind."

"This is serious," she said then, harshly. "I'm serious."

"Then get up, you fucking idiot," he growled, and her head shot up, her mouth dropping open in shock. "You heard me," he said when she only stared at him.

That color flooded her face again, and she rocked back against her heels, then up and onto her feet in a controlled kind of burst that was much more her than all the rest of this. It reminded him of the night she'd hit him, and he wanted that back. He wanted *her* back.

"I obviously made a much bigger mistake in coming here than I did in leaving in the first place," she said tightly, but at least that was a tone he recognized, cool and sharp. "Excuse me."

"Oh, no," he threw right back at her. "You don't get off that easy. What did you think would happen here? That I'd enjoy watching you sacrifice yourself to me? That that's even remotely what I want from you?"

"I have no idea what you want."

"You," he roared at her, glad when she jumped a little bit, when he could hear it bounce back at him from the walls. "I want *you,* not this bullshit surrender. *I* don't think you're broken, Zoe. *I* don't think you're a stain on anything. You do."

She let out a sound like a gasp, as if she'd been wounded, but he kept going, realizing he'd moved toward her only when she put up her hand against his chest as if she needed to ward him off. He stopped, but she didn't drop her hand, and he felt that touch—her palm searing through his shirt like an iron brand—all the way to his toes.

"Be the woman who challenged me out of a lifetime of self-pity," he told her, love and fury and need indistinguishable from each other in his voice, in the way he looked at her, in the self-control it took to keep from touching her, kissing her, finding her again in a more direct way than these words. But he couldn't do that.

"Hunter," she said, but he ignored her.

"Be my equal, the woman who knows that if she's damaged, then Jesus Christ, so am I. Be worth feeling all of this *crap,* Zoe." He could taste the ferocity on his own lips, copper like blood. "I want *you,* not whatever this is, that you can hide behind when it gets tough. You're not a martyr and I'm not a hero. Let's be who we are."

He was breathing hard, as if he was running, and she was, too, and he didn't know when that turmoil he'd seen in her eyes, across her face, had spilled out into tears. He couldn't keep himself from reaching over and brushing the moisture away with his thumbs, and she shuddered.

"I want everything," he told her, hoarse and sure. "Give me that, Zoe, or don't waste my time."

He saw the fight in her, the battle and the darkness and the fear, but she was so brave. So deeply courageous that he thought it might crack him wide open where he stood, and when her hands moved to hold his where they'd rested on either side of her face, something in him eased. Hoped.

"I don't know how," she whispered. "I don't know if I'll ever have *everything.* I don't know how to start."

"This is starting," he told her. "This is what it looks like. If it was easy, everyone would be a whole lot happier."

"Do you think that's possible?" she asked, and he knew it was a serious question, maybe the most serious she could ask him.

He kissed her then, long and sweet, a promise and a wish.

"For us?" he asked when he pulled away. "I think it's inevitable."

"What if I let you down? What if you wake up one morning and can't live with what I am?" She scowled at him, even though she clung to him. "And don't tell me that's not going to happen. It *could*. It *might*."

"Zoe," he said, matter-of-factly and brisk, never looking away from her. "We slay monsters. That's what we do. Even if those monsters are our own."

She studied him for the longest moment of his life. The most important moment, and then her face cleared, and she smiled.

It was the most beautiful thing he'd ever seen. She was.

"I love you," she said then. "I didn't think I should. I didn't think—"

"I know," he retorted. "But don't worry. I know exactly how I'll let you make it up to me. Prepare yourself, Zoe. It's going to be a long and arduous journey. It could take years."

That smile of hers tipped over into more of that edgy, dangerous smirk he loved more than anything, and it sparked inside him, hot and sexy, just like her.

"I can prove it in all of five seconds, if you lock that door."

"*Years,*" he said again. "Long years. With begging that does not involve martyrdom of any kind. And I was serious about the crawling."

"Oh, good," she murmured. "A challenge. Make that three seconds."

She took his mouth, or he took hers, and for a moment there was nothing but that fire of theirs, that glorious heat. *Them,* at last.

Then she pulled away, nipping him slightly on the lower lip as she went, the curve of her mouth enough to drive him wild, and she looked at him as if he were a miracle after all.

"Well?" she asked, taunting him, loving him. *His.* "Are you going to lock that door or am I?"

Some nights later, Zoe couldn't sleep.

She lay in Hunter's massive bed, the city lights arrayed above her like her own, personal Sistine Chapel. She was replete, even happy, though she hardly dared call it that. What Hunter could do to her with his talented, clever hands ought to have been illegal. She wasn't sure she'd care too much if it was, as long as he kept doing it.

Not that everything was about sex. There was the way he looked at her, as if he truly did cherish her, the way she'd imagined he might that morning in his kitchen. There was that kernel of hope inside her that grew a little bit bigger every day. That let her smile wider, enjoy him, enjoy *this.* That let her worry less about the things that she thought she lacked, and think more about the ways they seemed to fit together.

Very much as if they'd been waiting for each other through all these dark years.

As if dawn had finally come, for both of them.

He shifted, pulling her to him so her head was pillowed on his shoulder, then smoothing her hair away from her face.

"What is it?" His voice was a rasp in the dark. "You're still vibrating with tension, and without flattering myself too much, I think we both know that should be impossible."

She smiled. "I don't know. Maybe you're slipping?"

Hunter snorted as if *that* was impossible. Then he let out a long-suffering sigh.

"Fine," he said, as if they'd been arguing for hours. "What will make you happy? Do you need to paint every wall in this penthouse so it doesn't look like—what did you call it?"

"Abattoir chic?" she asked idly, grinning as she remembered the look of outrage on his face when she'd said it earlier. And his earthy response had involved her hands flat against the windows in his living room and him hard and hot behind her, then deep inside her.

"I'll stop fighting the inevitable," he said now. "Just promise me it won't be pastels."

She twisted around to look at him.

"That's not a bad idea," she said, as if he'd been serious. "You're not in purgatory anymore, Hunter. You didn't die ten years ago. You deserve to *live.*"

His face was shadowed but she still felt the impact of that bright, blue stare. She felt his big hand clutch her shoulder briefly, then return to its lazy smoothing, up and down her back.

"So do you," he said gruffly.

Zoe thought about what he'd said to her over and over

again in these wild, beautiful days she still couldn't quite believe were real. That they could replace dark memories with new and better fantasies. And it clicked into place then. Just like that. Maybe it had always been inevitable. Maybe she'd been waiting for this. This…happiness, if that was what this was. It was still new, but it didn't feel fragile. She didn't think the wrong word or moment or fight could dislodge it.

She wasn't sure anything could. It felt *right*.

Hunter didn't think she was an unpleasant duty the way her grandparents had. She knew he wouldn't turn on her and abuse her, as Jason Treffen had. Hadn't he proved it to her when she'd knelt down before him and he'd refused to accept that?

He didn't want to own her. He wanted to love her.

And that changed everything. It set her free, in all the ways she hadn't understood she wasn't when she'd ousted Jason Treffen from that law firm. Because this time, the fear wouldn't stop her. This time, she knew enough to let Hunter help her.

"I think I have to do it," she said then, in a rush. She felt Hunter tense beneath her, and flattened her hands against his smooth, hard chest. "Not because anyone expects it of me, or because Alex thinks it's a good idea to have one of the victims take part in the interview. But because I have to do it *for me*. Because I want to."

He was quiet, but she knew he was as focused on her as when he was deep inside her, when all that mattered was the heat and that fire, that beautiful dance that was only theirs. More, perhaps.

"You don't have to be a part of it," she told him quickly. "I'll understand if you don't want—"

"Zoe."

"It will probably get ugly," she continued doggedly, because she still wanted to protect him. He'd started new relationships with his family. He was teaching those kids football. He really was a good man now, a new man, and she was still a scandal. Likely a big one, if Alex had his way. "I'll be called a lot of names. So will you. People don't like it when their heroes get pushed off of pedestals, especially not when the pusher can be dismissed as a grasping whore. And I will be."

"Please shut up," he said. "I'm not having this conversation. And I'm not going anywhere. I told you." He took her chin in his hand, his thumb rubbing over her lips, possessive and hot and somehow deeply comforting, too. "I'll never stop wanting you, Zoe. This is a done deal."

After a moment, he let her go, and Zoe let herself breathe.

"In a few months, maybe three, I'm going to propose," he told her in the quiet that surrounded them, and she could hear his smile in the dark. As good as a light. "I'm telling you now so you can start preparing yourself."

"Propose what? Sexcapades? We already have those, don't we?"

He smacked her on her bottom, hard enough to make her laugh.

"Marriage," he said. "I figure you'll turn me down at least three times. Fear, disbelief, some misbegotten notion that I shouldn't tie myself down to someone like you. I'll offer to come up with a binding prenuptial agreement, which will enrage you, and you'll accept my loving proposal by doing something insane, like punching me, probably in public. I can't wait."

"Idiot," she muttered, but she was grinning. She crawled up over his perfectly sculpted chest and kissed him, hard. Then again, the way, she thought, she planned to keep right on doing for the rest of their lives.

"Is it three months yet?" he asked when she pulled away.

"Not yet," she said against his mouth. "You don't want to say anything too crazy tonight, Hunter. It could ruin the whole thing. Scare me off."

One of his hands came up and fisted in her hair, and she shivered, wanting him as desperately as she always did. More, because every day now, she trusted him more.

And the more she trusted him, the more she trusted herself, too.

"Then we better practice," he murmured against her mouth, and that easily, she was needy. Hungry. "So we're ready when the time comes."

They went together.

"Do you want to go in alone?" he asked when they were outside the office where, Zoe knew, Alex waited for them. Where she would tell her story in all its sordid, uncompromising detail, and make herself a very pointed nail in Jason Treffen's coffin.

She felt that panic again. She swallowed hard, searching his face.

"I don't want—"

"I swear to God," he said, his voice impatient but his blue eyes kind, so kind it made a lump swell in her throat, "if you say anything to me about the things you think I don't want to hear—"

"You won't want to hear them," she said fiercely.

"No," he said evenly, his gaze never wavering. "I won't. Because I love you, Zoe, and I will marry you no matter how many times you freak out about it, and I'll hate every second of this because I hate that you had to live through it. But you did. And look at you. You're a wonder. The most amazing woman I've ever known. If you can sit and tell your story, if you can go on national television and accuse Jason to his face, then I can sit with you and hear that story. I can share the burden." His beautiful mouth crooked. "Or try. I'd like to try."

She was overwhelmed. Tears pricked at the back of her eyes and she didn't care if they fell.

"I love you, too," she whispered.

That grin of his deepened, went cocky. As if he'd always known it would end this way, that he'd win. But then again, maybe she had, too. Maybe they both had.

Maybe that was the point.

"Bring it on," he said, the way she'd known he would, like he was looking forward to a good fight.

It turned out she was, too.

And Zoe opened the door, but they walked through it together.

★ ★ ★ ★ ★

Hunter reached over and tucked a strand of [hair be]hind her ear, and then he waited.

Zoe looked at Alex's door, and pulled in a de[ep, hard] breath. To mark this momentous occasion, her out[fit as] one of "Jason's girls," she'd worn white. Crisp white j[eans] and a flowing cream top. Virginal and pure. She'd se[en] Hunter's smile when she'd emerged from her bedroom this morning, and she'd known the symbolism wasn't lost on him.

Because she might be about to tell the hardest story she knew, to a man who would use it as a weapon to take down the monster who'd tortured her for over a decade, but she still knew PR. She could spin anything. Even this.

She'd always wanted revenge on Jason Treffen, but this was better. This would be justice.

"I'm ready," she said.

Hunter stood beside her like a bodyguard. The wall between her and the world that she didn't need to carry around inside herself any longer, because he'd do it instead. He'd be her shield, just as she'd be his.

They deserved a future free of the past. Free of ghosts. *Free.*

And there was only one way to do that.

"This might get a little bit crazy," she warned him again, for the last time, and he only smiled, then reached over and took her hand, lacing his fingers through hers.

As if they were one unit, one thought. *One.*

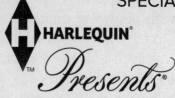
* * *

"You sound like you hate the man."

"*Hate* isn't the right word. But I'd like to see what he does
with an interview. What you do with it." He raised his beer bottle
to his lips, his eyes hard.

She straightened, flashed him one of her glittering smiles.
"Well, stay tuned, then. It airs live on March twentieth." And
without waiting for a response, she turned and walked away from
him, her shoulders thrown back, her chin held high.

Alex watched her leave. For a moment there he'd considered
telling her the truth about Jason Treffen, but then he'd thankfully
thought better of it. It was hardly cocktail party chitchat, and
he didn't know her well enough to trust her with that particular
powder keg. Not yet, anyway.

She was ambitious, he got that, and tough. He was pretty sure
she had the balls to bring down Treffen on live television if she
wanted to.

The question was, did she? Could he convince her? He possessed a savage need to see Treffen with his world crumbling around him while everyone else saw it, too. No longer would the man fool everyone into believing he was such a damned saint. They would know him not just as a sinner, but as a devil.

Austin had already exposed Treffen to his family with the help of Sarah's sister, Katy. Hunter was working on ousting Treffen from his law firm. And Alex had been charged with showing the world what he really was: a monster who used the women he claimed to be saving. Who damned them to lives of shame, scandal and sin. Everything in Alex ached to see Jason publicly exposed—and he would do whatever it took to make it happen.

Including use Chelsea in whatever way he could. The woman was cold. He didn't feel so much as a flicker of guilt for using her. But he did feel a certain amount of frustration. *Sexual* frustration. He wanted Chelsea Maxwell in bed, beneath him, those gray-green eyes turned to molten-silver with desire. He wanted her haughty little smile to become a desperate begging kiss, to turn her tinkling laugh into a breathy sigh of pleasure and need.

He wanted to be the one to do it. To shatter her icy control and make her melt. For him.

* * *

*The third and final step to revenge in the **Fifth Avenue** trilogy.*
Alex has the power...
August 2014

HARLEQUIN®
Presents®

Revenge and seduction intertwine...

Behind the Scenes of *Fifth Avenue:*
Read on for an exclusive interview with Maisey Yates!

It's such an exciting world to create. Did you discuss it with the other writers?
There was a lot of discussion! Thankfully we live in a world of Skype and FaceTime and we were able to spend time not just emailing, but having face-to-face discussions, in spite of the fact that we're in different states and countries. I love technology.

How does writing a trilogy with other authors differ from when you are writing your own stories?
Kate and Caitlin are not just fantastic writers, but they're friends as well, which made collaboration and communication so much easier. There's a fine balance to constructing a series that will have different elements executed by different authors. I'm used to focusing on an individual book, but in this case a broader awareness was required.

What was the biggest challenge? And what did you most enjoy about it?
I think the biggest challenge was pinpointing which series elements needed to happen in which book. There has to be excitement and new revelations in every installment of the series, and making those decisions was tricky! I think what I most enjoyed was brainstorming as a group. Watching this germ of an idea expand and grow. We each brought a unique perspective to the overall series, which created something I'm not sure would have been possible if we'd simply tackled it as individuals.

As you wrote your hero and heroine was there anything about them that surprised you?
I think Austin surprised me the most. He has such a huge amount of decency, and so many ideas about what it means to be a good man. Which is why he's so conflicted by what he sees as "dark desires." They don't mesh with who he thinks he should be. But even I was surprised by the full intensity that he had hidden beneath his suit!

What was your favourite part of creating the world of *Fifth Avenue?*
I love the idea that such a beautiful world, insulated by money and power, could be hiding something so dark. I think digging in and exposing all the ugliness beneath the glitter, and really going for the scandal, was so much fun!

If you could have given your heroine one piece of advice before the opening pages of the book, what would it be?
Probably DON'T sleep with your mortal enemy's son. (Katy says: But he's superhot and good with a tie. Me: I retract my advice.)

What was your hero's biggest secret?
A lot of the secrets in the book belong to other people. Austin is, in many ways, kind of a normal guy (for a billionaire philanthropist). But I think his biggest secret is what he really craves from a sexual partner. He was even lying to himself about it! Until Katy.

What does your hero love most about your heroine?
Her strength. She's been through hell and never stops pushing, never stops pursuing justice for her sister, and a better life for her brother.

What does your heroine love most about your hero?
I think Austin restored her faith in people. And in love.

Which of your *Fifth Avenue* characters would you most like to meet and why?
I'll be very simple and say Austin. Who doesn't love a hot man in a suit?

HPQA0614TR

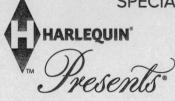
* * *

KATY let out a long breath and started walking back down the empty corridor, back to the party.

Back toward Jason Treffen.

Talking to him had just about made her lose her mind. It had taken everything in her not to grab his glass from his hand and pour it over his head. Then break the glass on his face.

She considered the man as good as her sister's murderer, so she was short on charitable feelings where he was concerned.

The door to the ballroom opened, and she froze.

Oh. Her breath left her in a rush, a current of electricity washing over her skin.

It was him.

The man whose eyes were like an endless black hole, drawing her in, a force she couldn't deny or control. When he had looked at her, she'd felt as if she were grounded to the spot. She'd felt like he had looked and *seen* her.

Seen everything. More than that, she'd looked back and she'd seen him.

Had seen a grief in him. An anger.

It had been, in some ways, like looking into a mirror.

"It's you," he said, his voice deep, smooth. Like really good chocolate. "I was hoping to run into you."

"Wh-why were you hoping to run into me?" she asked.

"Because you're the most beautiful woman here. Why wouldn't I want to see you?"

"You're a flirt."

"That's the thing, I'm not really." He put his hands in his pockets, a wicked half smile curling that sinful mouth.

"I have to get back."

She started to walk past him and he took her arm, stopped her progress. She looked up and met cold, dark eyes.

"To who?" he asked, his voice gentle, an opposing force to the hold he had on her.

There was something about that grip. Commanding. It spoke to every secret fantasy that lived in the dark shadows inside her. The parts of herself that had looked at every man she'd even tried to date and found them lacking.

But not him. He wouldn't be lacking. Something shivered inside her, a whisper.

He would know what you wanted.

* * *

*The first step to revenge in the **Fifth Avenue** trilogy*
Austin has the plan...
June 2014

HARLEQUIN®

Presents®

Harlequin Presents welcomes you to
the world of **The Chatsfield;**

Synonymous with style, spectacle…and scandal!

SHEIKH'S SCANDAL by *Lucy Monroe* (May 2014)

PLAYBOY'S LESSON by *Melanie Milburne* (June 2014)

SOCIALITE'S GAMBLE by *Michelle Conder* (July 2014)

BILLIONAIRE'S SECRET by *Chantelle Shaw* (August 2014)

TYCOON'S TEMPTATION by *Trish Morey* (September 2014)

RIVAL'S CHALLENGE by *Abby Green* (October 2014)

REBEL'S BARGAIN by *Annie West* (November 2014)

HEIRESS'S DEFIANCE by *Lynn Raye Harris* (December 2014)

Step into the gilded world of **The Chatsfield!**
Where secrets and scandal lurk behind every door…

Reserve your room!
June 2014

www.Harlequin.com